Chekhov's *Three Sisters*
AND
Woolf's *Orlando*

Books by Sarah Ruhl available from TCG

Chekhov's *Three Sisters* and Woolf's *Orlando*
(two renderings for the stage)

The Clean House and Other Plays
INCLUDES:
The Clean House
Eurydice
Late: a cowboy song
Melancholy Play

Dead Man's Cell Phone

In the Next Room or the vibrator play

Passion Play

Chekhov's *Three Sisters*

AND

Woolf's *Orlando*

TWO RENDERINGS FOR THE STAGE

By Sarah Ruhl

THEATRE COMMUNICATIONS GROUP
NEW YORK
2013

The publication of *Chekhov's Three Sisters and Woolf's Orlando: Two Renderings for the Stage*, by Sarah Ruhl, through TCG's Book Program, is made possible in part by the New York State Council on the Arts with the support of Governor Andrew Cuomo and the New York State Legislature.

TCG books are exclusively distributed to the book trade by Consortium Book Sales and Distribution.

LIBRARY OF CONGRESS CATALOGING-IN-PUBLICATION DATA
Ruhl, Sarah, 1974–
Chekhov's Three Sisters and Woolf's Orlando : two renderings for the stage / by Sarah Ruhl.
pages cm
ISBN 978-1-55936-404-1 (trade paper)
I. Chekhov, Anton Pavlovich, 1860–1904. Tri sestry. English. II. Woolf, Virginia, 1882–1941. Orlando. III. Title.
PS3618.U48C48   2013
812'.6—dc23   2013001992

Book design and composition by Lisa Govan

Cover art and design by Barbara de Wilde

First Edition, April 2013

For Joyce Piven,
who teaches generations of children
how to change forms

Contents

When Woolf Saw Chekhov,
something of an introduction

On another evening Vita and Virginia went to see *Three Sisters* and then called in on Dotty in her flat in Mount Street, who was lying asleep and "woke up chattering & hysterical. Virginia Woolf Virginia Woolf My God! Virginia Woolf is in the room. For Gods Sake Vita don't turn the lights on . . . We sat and drank."

—Virginia Woolf, Hermione Lee, p. 498

It is perhaps an unimportant fact that Virginia Woolf and Vita Sackville-West went to see *Three Sisters* together one evening in London. The event could be a completely arbitrary (although tempting) justification for including *Orlando* and *Three Sisters* in one volume together, although truly, I put them in the same volume because I wrote neither one and my betters wrote both and in that sense they seemed to belong together.

Still, imagine: Virginia Woolf and Vita Sackville-West went to see *Three Sisters* together one evening in London. Was the night rainy, was it pitch black? Did they weep at the end of the play, did they sigh, did they rise to their feet? Perhaps Virginia was too English to weep in public; perhaps the performance did not merit weeping. Perhaps she turned to Vita and merely raised one eyebrow. Perhaps she commented on the slightness of the translation. We will never know. At any rate, after sighing or weeping or neither, Vita and Virginia left the theater and then called on "Dotty" who was lying asleep and then became hysterical upon seeing Virginia Woolf. Then the three women, these three women, sat and drank with the lights off.

What did Woolf and Sackville-West make of *Three Sisters*, and why should it matter? And what do Virginia Woolf and Anton Chekhov have in common? For one thing, I think they were much funnier than we ordinarily take them for. They were of the nineteenth century and yet they formally destroyed the nineteenth century. They were both childless and sickly and wrote in many genres. They both died too young. They knew aristocrats but were not themselves born into the aristocracy. They were acute observers of that elusive thing called human nature, and they were not content to write about this or that issue, or this or that person—they wrote about the whole experience, they wrote about being. They constantly redirect the reader to the present moment of experience, rather than relying on the easy clean sweep of an arc.

Walter Pater, one of Woolf's favorite critics, wrote in *The Renaissance*:

> Every moment some form grows perfect in hand or face; some tone on the hills or the sea is choicer than the rest; some mood of passion or insight or intellectual excitement is irresistibly real and attractive to us—for that moment only . . . Not the fruit of experience, but experience itself, is the end. Not to discriminate every moment some passionate attitude in those about us . . . is to sleep before evening. With this sense of the splendor of our experience and of its awful brevity, gathering all we are into one desperate effort to see and touch, we shall hardly have time to make theories about the things we see and touch.

It is as though Pater's rallying cry is also Woolf's rallying cry—that experience itself, rather than the fruit of experience, is the end. One might imagine *Three Sisters'* resident philosopher Vershinin philosophizing right along with Pater, but coming to a different conclusion. Vershinin believed in progress, and I'm not sure that Woolf did.

Both Woolf and Chekhov land, in the end, on the epiphany that never quite comes. Woolf once said that the only thing she knew about the ending of *Orlando* was that it would end in an ellipsis . . . The manuscript version does end with ". . ." but the published version does not. (Perhaps it is difficult in publication to end in an ellipsis, as publication implies closure and finality.) At any rate, in this adaptation, I attempted to go back to Woolf's original intention and ended with a dot dot dot. I went back to the moment in the novel when Orlando says: "I am *about* to understand . . ." We are never quite sure if our hero/heroine makes it through the threshold to understanding, just as we don't quite know the outcome of Olga's last wish, "To know, to know!"

Virginia Woolf says of Chekhov in *The Common Reader*:

> Our first impressions of Chekhov are not of simplicity but of bewilderment. What is the point of it, and why does he make a story out of this? we ask as we read story after story . . . But is it the end, we ask? We have rather the feeling that we have overrun our signals; or it is as if a tune had stopped short without the expected chords to close it. These stories are inconclusive, we say, and proceed to frame a criticism based upon the assumption that stories ought to conclude in a way that we recognize. In so doing, we raise the question of our own fitness as readers. Where the tune is familiar and the end emphatic—lovers united, villains discomfited, intrigues exposed—as it is in most Victorian fiction, we can scarcely go wrong, but where the tune is unfamiliar and the end a note of interrogation or merely the information that they went on talking, as it is in Chekhov, we need a very daring and alert sense of literature to make

us hear the tune, and in particular those last notes which complete the harmony . . . As we read these little stories about nothing at all, the horizon widens; the soul gains an astonishing sense of freedom. In reading Chekhov we find ourselves repeating the word "soul" again and again. It sprinkles his pages . . . perhaps that is why it needs so great an effort on the part of an English reader to read *The Brothers Karamzov* . . . The "soul" is alien to him. It is even antipathetic. It has little sense of humor and no sense of comedy. It is formless.

I too remember struggling with the word "soul" when I translated *Three Sisters*. The word seems to come out of the Russian mouth with less effort; out of an American actor's mouth, the word "soul" dangles. But I used it anyway, to be faithful, and both of the following adaptations are nothing if not faithful. The formless nature of the soul, and the formless nature of consciousness, seem equally important to Woolf and to Chekhov, who both seemed to ask: what aesthetic form might consciousness take? What if plot (like the body in *Orlando*) is a rather insignificant and illusory trapping that can be dispensed with?

In the American theater, we still have our Victorian fictions— the lovers united, villains discomfited and intrigues exposed. But what happens in the theater when the last notes which complete the harmony are somewhat incomplete? And I think it is no accident that Woolf used the metaphor of music when trying to describe Chekhov's form. It is almost as though he was writing linguistic music—the note completes the play rather than a thesis or a duel, in the same way that Woolf's linguistic rhythm made its own kind of meaning, mirroring the speed of the interior, rather than describing living rooms.

My beloved Belgian, Maurice Maeterlinck, another writer unafraid of the soul, wrote in "The Tragical in Daily Life":

There is a tragic element in the life of every day that is far more real, far more penetrating, far more akin to the true self that is in us than the tragedy that lies in great adventure . . . It goes beyond the determined struggle of man against man, and desire against desire . . . Its province is rather to reveal to us how truly wonderful is the mere act of living, and to throw light upon the existence of the soul . . . Indeed, when I go to a theater, I feel as though I were spending a few hours with my ancestors, who conceived life as something that was primitive, arid and brutal . . . I am shown a deceived husband killing his wife . . . murdered kings, ravished virgins, imprisoned citizens . . . I had hoped to be shown some act of life, traced back to its sources and to its mystery . . . I shall be told, perhaps, that a motionless life would be invisible, that therefore animation must be conferred upon it . . .

Woolf and Chekhov, chasing illumination over and above animation, trying to capture the invisible moments as they fled, I humbly kneel before you. I am sorry to squeeze you together into one volume, to make false comparisons between you, to squeeze you, Ms. Woolf, onto the vulgar smallness of the stage, and to squeeze you, Mr. Chekhov, into the vulgar smallness of the English language. I did what I did with the tools that I have and I hope that you forgive me, and I hope that somewhere you are looking down on all of us and laughing, as you contemplate the illusory nature of endings.

—Sarah Ruhl
New York
December 2012

Three Sisters

By Anton Chekhov

English Version by Sarah Ruhl

BASED ON A LITERAL TRANSLATION BY

Elise Thoron with Natasha Paramonova
and Kristin Johnsen-Neshati

For my sister Kate

Author's Notes

When Cincinnati Playhouse approached me to translate *Three Sisters* I was both terrified and happy. Terrified, because I don't speak Russian and I love the play; happy, because I don't speak Russian and I love the play. As such, I thought: I will learn from a great master, and I will try to learn Russian, a language I have always wanted to learn. They said: we need it in six months. So I thought: I won't learn Russian. But I will learn from a great master, with some help. As it turns out, quite a lot of help. Let me explain about all of my help.

The night before I first met John Doyle, the director of the project, I was at a fundraiser. My husband and I were seated with New York business moguls who often attend fundraisers. I glanced to my left. Three chairs down was a woman wearing a flowing red silk shirt, and she had very long tapered fingers. The hands of a poet, I thought. She didn't exactly look bored, but she looked intriguing. Who is this woman? I must move chairs, I thought. I moved chairs over dessert. It turns out the woman was a Russian scholar and an extraordinary playwright/director named Elise Thoron. We got to talking about Chekhov and his luminosity, transparency, and spareness, which is often lost in translation. It was serendipity. After I met with John, I asked if Elise could come on as my Russian language conduit. He, and the theater, happily agreed.

Meanwhile, I went to Los Angeles for a family vacation where my in-laws live. My sister-in-law Natasha who is a native Russian speaker sat down with me and read to me from the original. We sat on her stoop while her baby slept and while her twelve-year-old daughter Masha showed us Tae Kwan Do kicks. That Masha asked: what did the other Masha say? Natasha gave me literal translations of the idioms—as when Solyony says: pull my finger, meaning, just as it does in this country, make me fart, which the more polite translations usually cover, making Solyony seem completely opaque. Or when Masha says: Life is a raspberry! I wanted to keep the raspberry, even though it's not readily accessible in English. Working with Natasha, it became clear to me that getting to the root of the original Russian was what I wanted, rather than putting my own authorial stamp on the text. I wanted to get as far away from a "stamp" as possible. I desperately needed a native speaker for things like: a word in act four that could either mean "a metal lid on top of steaming food" or "the kind of hat an entertainer would wear when performing for a czar."

Not speaking Russian and translating Chekhov, is of course, a terrible disadvantage. Luckily I had four very able helpers. Cincinnati Playhouse procured for me a translation to look at, by Kristin Johnsen-Neshati. It is a lovely translation, clear and modern, and was very useful to read in the early stages of my work. Because it is a wonderful translation in its own right, and not literal, I couldn't work directly from it. Still, it was a valuable tool for comparison, as was Stark Young's translation; and his, I think, is one of the closest in English to the literal Russian in terms of content, rhythm and punctuation.

After being in Los Angeles, I happened to be in Chicago, where I'm from, and where I talked at length with a teacher from childhood, Joyce Piven. I had adapted two Chekhov short stories with Joyce, and she's directed and studied Chekhov all her life. We drank tea, and talked about *Three Sisters* in her living room. Joyce studied acting in New York in the sixties with a woman named Mira Rostova, the great Russian acting teacher who taught the likes of Uta Hagen. Rostova divided speech into five melodies, called "the doings." One was the "lament with humor." Chekhov's work is full of laments with humor—the philosophical shrug of the shoulders and sigh that the oppressed people of the world know so well—it is the "ah, well" in the bars in Ireland, it is the "so, nu?" in Yiddish. It is the acceptance of fate, a beautiful forbearance with a touch of philosophical humor that seems so rare in America at times. It is ancient. Many Americans' first impulse, I fear, when struck with bad luck, is to complain rather than to lament. The lament contains acceptance, a "what can you do but laugh," whereas the complaint implies the measured control of the people who expanded westward: "how dare life do this to me, feel sorry for me, no one should give me a raw deal, I'm an American, I can change my fate." The melody of complaint comes through the nasal passages, "I didn't get what I wanted." The complaint should, I feel, be avoided at all costs in most theater but especially in Chekhov where there is such danger of it becoming the emotional vernacular of the play.

In Rostova and Piven's melodies, the "defy" also looms large. The classic defy is Shakespeare's: "Once more into the breach!" Rostova and Piven's notion is that playwrights' words have natural emotional and melodic rhythms that should be respected, rather than imposing bizarre "line readings" onto the line; for example, turning the natural sweep of "once more into the breach!" into "once more—into the breach?" I think Olga, Irina and Masha are often defying their fate ("To Moscow!") rather than complaining about their fate, and this assumption often dictated my choice in translation. For example, many translate the very last line of the play as: "if only we knew, if only we knew." In the literal Russian there is no pronoun (as there often isn't in the Russian) and it's not necessarily past tense. So I chose to translate the phrase as: "To know, to know!" which is a defy rather than a lament, and is certainly not a complaint. To look for the act of defiance in the sisters rather than the elegy; to find the philosophical lament with humor rather than the complaint . . . this was my hope in the translation, and also my hope with the actors who ultimately do the production.

I came to this translation with no agenda, no desire to bend Chekhov to my will in any way, but instead, to learn from him. It is, then, a very faithful translation, phrase by phrase, stage direction by stage direction, comma by comma. I tried to cleave to Chekhov's original rhythms as far as I was able to. Sometimes that involved leaving out pronouns in the English where you might normally see them. For example, in one of Irina's speeches, many translations use "I am crying" rather than, as in the literal Russian, "tears are flowing." "I am crying" implies bodily agency, self-pity, and self-awareness; whereas "tears are flowing" is a sudden *discovery* of a condition. And the discovery is another melody, another vital doing in Rostova and Piven's schema. I think much of the humor of the play comes from the moment to moment discovery of emotional states, though the play is often understood in terms of the lyricism of looking backward. Instead, the sisters are constantly discovering in the moment that they will not go to Moscow. They never know it ahead of time. And they keep forgetting, over and over, only to discover the same reality in the next act.

The emphasis in the Russian is on the noun "tears," or "Moscow," on the event, the discovery, rather than on the subject "I," the self-reflexive emotion. People watching themselves emote and describing their own emoting with an "I" or a "my" seems more culturally American, and more contemporary. The flipside of the lack of solipsism in the Russian language is the possible abdication of responsibility, emotionally or otherwise, when one omits the "I." In terms of articles absconding . . . when Olga describes her headache, she is often translated as saying "my head, my head" when in the literal Russian her language is more fragmented, without an article, as in "head, head." One can imagine having a terrible headache and omitting articles. Rather than smoothing out or trying to make the language more logical, I tried to respect the breakages, disjunctions, oddness, and fragmentation that I think Chekhov was purposely working toward, as an expression of character, event or life view. His stage directions are almost all intact, particularly the odder ones, such as when Andrei "almost threatens the audience with his fists," so that productions can freely depart from the original, but they'll know what the original was.

I occasionally included words in the original Russian, to give the actors the flavor of the words inside their mouths, which I think would make their faces move more, and make their inner lives more suitable for Chekhov; and also because I think English is a terrible jackhammer for terms of endearment. Why say "dear

Masha" when you could say "Milya Masha." Why say "my little dove" when you could say "galupchik moi." Poor English. Poor sad impoverished English with our lack of "ushas" and "itas" to endear ourselves, to play with, the names of our beloveds. Oh, and one note on my use of line breaks. Chekhov doesn't often use line breaks in his text in the way that I do—it is probably my only departure from the shape of the original. Because it is how I lay out my own plays in English, and how I see the way I hear the actors speak, I thought it would be useful for the actors to hear the rhythms in my head as I translated. But they aren't intended to indicate an overly poeticized approach, or epic pauses. They are more about the rhythm of thinking than anything.

One final note on Russian indifference and the phrase *vsyo ravno* (it's all the same, it's all equal, what's the difference, who cares), which appears dozens and dozens of times in the text. I feel that the phrase is intensely Russian and almost impossible to translate. I think the best cultural equivalent is perhaps Janis Joplin on "Ball and Chain" when she croons, "it's all the same fucking day, man." *Who cares* is too casual, *what's the difference* is too caustic and oddly engaged in its disengagement, and *it's all the same* seemed about right in terms of a mathematical equivalence, but I am quite sure it sounds different on the streets of Moscow. I was tempted to leave it in the original Russian but didn't want the audience to be entirely left out of Chekhov's struggle with the indifferent stance, which was philosophical, literary, and of the street, all at once. I tried my best. Or, to be more in keeping with the defy and present-tense of the three sisters, "I try!"

Huge thanks to Elise Thoron; there is not a more intelligent, graceful person of the theater, and I loved every minute of sitting in her apartment, drinking tea with jam, and hearing her speak the original cadences of the play. She went through every single word with me, and I am so grateful. Also many thanks to my sister-in-law Natasha Paramonova, who, when she is not helping me with *Three Sisters* is a brilliant nurse on a cardiac care unit and was almost a nuclear physicist; to her husband Marcus and my husband Tony for feeding the children while Natasha and I talked about the particular light in Moscow in the spring. Thanks also to Kristin Johnsen-Neshati, for letting me look at her manuscript early on in the process. I was also indebted to Stark Young for his faithfulness to the literal, Curt Columbus for sending me his translation, and Laurence Senelick for his careful scholarship. I would also like to thank all the actors who took the time to read the first two acts of the translation with me around a table; their insights were invaluable and cleared a path for me: Michael Cerveris, Felix Solis, Bray Poor, Ron and Lynn Cohen, Keith Reddin, Yusef Bulos, Gian-Murray Gianino, Thomas Jay Ryan, Marin Ireland, Kate Arrington, Maria Dizzia, Polly Noonan, Kathleen Tolan, Manoel Felciano. Thanks to Kate Pines and Stefan Rowny for listening. And thanks to John Steber and New Dramatists for providing space and support for the occasion.

The year after my father died, when I was on the strange boundary between childhood and adulthood, I lived in a house with my sister, in a province, you might say, of Chicago, longing to move to New York. I don't mean to say that I can fully understand what it was to live in provincial Russia; all I know is, at the time, I dreamed of birch trees. I don't pretend to be anything in this manuscript but Chekhov's student, and Chekhov's ridiculously English-speaking student. I am sorry, Anton, for any havoc I have wreaked, and I thank you for your plays, your life, for, without intending to, giving me the gift of sitting in my apartment, while it snowed, trying to translate the line: Look: it's snowing. What is the meaning of snow?

Sarah Ruhl
New York
July 2009

Three Sisters received its world premiere at Cincinnati Playhouse in the Park (Edward Stern, Producing Artistic Director; Buzz Ward, Executive Director) in Cincinnati, Ohio, on October 24, 2009. It was directed by John Doyle; the set design was by Scott Pask, the costume design was by Ann Hould-Ward, the lighting design was by Jane Cox, the sound design and original music were by Dan Moses Schreier; the dramaturg was Elise Thoron and the stage manager was Suann Pollock. The cast was:

OLGA	Alma Cuervo
MASHA	Laila Robins
IRINA	Hannah Cabell
ANDREI	Alexander Gemignani
NATASHA	Sarah Agnew
KULYGIN	Keith Reddin
VERSHININ	Corey Stoll
SOLYONY	Felix Solis
CHEBUTYKIN	Terry Greiss
TUZENBACH	Frank Wood
ANFISA	Lynn Cohen
FEDOTIK	Tim Abrahamsen
RODÉ	Joe Watts, Jr.
FERAPONT	Ronald Cohen
MAID	Kelly Pekar

Three Sisters opened at Piven Theatre Workshop (Byrne and Joyce Piven, Co-Founders; Joyce Piven, Artistic Director Emeritus) in Evanston, Illinois, on October 18, 2010. It was directed by Joyce Piven; the set design was by Aaron Menninga, the costume design was by Bill Morey, the lighting design was by Andrew Iverson, the sound design and original music were by Collin Warren; the dramaturg was Stephen Fedo and the production stage manager was Wendy Woodward. The cast was:

OLGA	Joanne Underwood
MASHA	Saren Nofs-Snyder
IRINA	Ravi Batista
ANDREI	Dave Belden
NATASHA	Amanda Hartley
KULYGIN	Brent T. Barnes
VERSHININ	Daniel Smith
SOLYONY	Jay Reed
CHEBUTYKIN	John Fenner Mays
TUZENBACH	Andy Hager
ANFISA	Kathleen Ruhl
FEDOTIK	Marcus Davis
RODÉ	Jacob Murphy
FERAPONT	Kevin D'Ambrosio

Three Sisters opened at Berkeley Repertory Theatre (Tony Taccone, Artistic Director; Susan Medak, Managing Director) in Berkeley, California, in co-production with Yale Repertory Theatre, on April 8, 2011. It was directed by Les Waters; the set design was by Annie Smart, the costume design was by Ilona Somogyi, the lighting design was by Alexander V. Nichols, the sound design was by David Budries; the dramaturg was Rachel Steinberg and the stage manager was Michael Suenkel. The cast was:

OLGA	Wendy Rich Stetson
MASHA	Natalia Payne
IRINA	Heather Wood
ANDREI	Alex Moggridge

NATASHA	Emily Kitchens
KULYGIN	Keith Reddin
VERSHININ	Bruce McKenzie
SOLYONY	Sam Breslin Wright
CHEBUTYKIN	James Carpenter
TUZENBACH	Thomas Jay Ryan
ANFISA	Barbara Oliver
FEDOTIK	David Abrams
RODÉ	Cobe Gordon
FERAPONT	Richard Farrell

The co-production opened at Yale Repertory Theatre (James Bundy, Artistic Director; Victoria Nolan, Managing Director) in New Haven, Connecticut, on September 16, 2011. All personnel were the same, with the following exceptions: the stage manager was James Mountcastle; Fedotik was played by Brian Wiles and Rodé was played by Josiah Bania.

CHARACTERS

The Prozorov Sisters:
   OLGA

   MASHA

   IRINA

ANDREI (their brother)

NATASHA (his wife)

KULYGIN (Masha's husband)

VERSHININ (a colonel)

SOLYONY (a staff captain)

CHEBUTYKIN (an army doctor)

TUZENBACH (a baron and lieutenant)

ANFISA (a nurse, eighty years old)

FEDOTIK (second lieutenant)

RODÉ (second lieutenant)

FERAPONT (an old watchman)

Act I

The Prozorovs' home.
A large room, with a living area and a dining area.
Midday.
Full of light.
A table is being set for lunch.

Olga, wearing a blue teacher's uniform, correcting student exams.
Masha, wearing black, her hat in her lap, reading a book.
Irina, in a white dress, stands, thinking.

OLGA

Father died a year ago today, on your birthday, Irina, May fifth.
It was so cold, it snowed.
I thought I'd never live through it, and you fainted, as though
you were the dead one.
But now it's been a year, and we can remember with some—
lightness.
You're wearing white again, and your face is shining.

The clock strikes twelve.

OLGA

The clock struck then too, on that day—it sounded like this.
I remember, when they carried Father away, the music playing.
And guns firing, at the cemetery.
He was a commander, of a whole troop—
still, not many people came. Well, it was raining—
freezing rain mixed in with snow.

IRINA

Why remember!

Tuzenbach, Chebutykin, and Solyony appear in the dining area.

OLGA

Today is warm, we can leave the windows wide open.
The birch trees are almost blooming.
I remember so clearly, eleven years ago, Father was an officer,
and we left Moscow, in early May, same as today.
Moscow in early May!—blooming, warm, golden.
Eleven years ago—but yesterday.
My God! I woke up this morning, saw masses of light flooding in,
and my God, the spring!
I felt this great happiness in my soul, and I wanted to go home.

CHEBUTYKIN

To hell with you both!

TUZENBACH

Fine, fine, it's silliness.

Masha whistles a tune.

OLGA

Stop whistling, Masha. It's bad luck.

Every day I teach, every night I tutor.
My head aches, always, and my thoughts are an old lady's.

16

Four years serving that school and I feel my youth and strength draining out of me.
The only thing that gets stronger is a dream—

IRINA

To go to Moscow! Sell the house, be done with everything, and go—

OLGA

Yes! Fast as we can, to Moscow.

Chebutykin and Tuzenbach laugh.

IRINA

Andrei will most likely be a professor, he won't stay in this town.
But poor Masha . . . stuck here . . .

OLGA

Masha can visit every summer.

Masha whistles.

IRINA

I hope so. *(She looks out the window)*
It's so beautiful out!
I don't know why I feel so happy!
This morning I thought: it's my birthday!
And suddenly I felt so happy, and I could feel my childhood, when Mama was alive.
And I thought happier and happier thoughts, coming at me like waves, oh what thoughts!

OLGA

Today all of you is shining, you're prettier than ever.
Masha looks pretty too.
Andrei would be nice-looking; only he's gotten so fat, doesn't look good on him.
And I got old, bony—it's because of the girls at school,
I get so angry.

17

But today I'm free, I'm home! My head doesn't hurt, and I feel younger than I did yesterday. Maybe everything is for the best, God's will and all that, but I do think if I'd gotten married and sat home all day, it would have been nicer.

I would have loved my husband.

TUZENBACH

(To Solyony) You say such stupid things, I won't listen.

Tuzenbach enters.

TUZENBACH

I forgot to tell you; today, you will have a visit from our new commanding officer. Colonel Vershinin.

Tuzenbach sits down at the piano.

OLGA

Really? That's nice.

IRINA

Is he old?

TUZENBACH

Not so much. Forty, forty-five at the outer limit.

He plays the piano.

TUZENBACH

Seems like a good man. And not stupid. Without a doubt. But he does talk. A lot.

IRINA

Is he interesting?

TUZENBACH

Mm—Sure. But he has a wife, and a mother-in-law to go with her, and two little girls. On top of that, it's his *second* wife. He goes around saying: I have a wife and two girls. He'll tell you too. But his wife is sad and half-crazy, wears her hair in long braids like a child, talks in overblown language about "philosophy," and frequently tries to kill herself. She likes to add salt to his already existing wounds, I suppose. I would have left a woman like that years ago, but he's a stoic—he stays and complains.

SOLYONY

(Crossing from dining room to living room with Chebutykin) I can only lift fifty pounds with one arm, but I can lift two hundred pounds with two arms. What do I conclude? That two men are twice as strong as one, or three times even, or more . . .

CHEBUTYKIN

(Reads a newspaper while walking) A remedy for hair loss: mix two ounces of naphthalene in a bottle of alcohol. Dissolve and use daily. I'll make a note of that in my little book! *(Makes a note in his book. Then, to Solyony)* Here's what you do. Take a cork, stick it in a bottle, get a glass pipe, put it through the cork. Then take a pinch of baking soda—

IRINA

Ivan Romanych, my dear Ivan Romanych!

CHEBUTYKIN

What is it, my girl, my joy?

IRINA

Tell me why I'm so happy today!
I'm a ship with sails, full sails,
and the sky over me blue and wide,
and full of birds!
Big white birds!
Why do you think that is?
Why?

CHEBUTYKIN

(Kissing her hands) My white bird.

19

IRINA

I woke up this morning, got up and washed my face,
and everything in the world seemed suddenly clear to me,
and I knew how to live.
I knew everything!
Sweet Ivan Romanych!
People have to work, to *labor*!
Work by the sweat of our brows.
No matter who we are. This is our one purpose, joy, ecstasy!
The thrill of getting up in the morning and drilling a hole in the
street! Or feeding sheep, or teaching children, or, or—making a
train go!
My God! Why be a person? I'd rather be an ox—or a simple
horse—and *do* something!—
Anything but a young lady, who wakes at noon, drinks her coffee
in bed, and takes two hours to button a dress.
Disgusting!
I want to work the way I want an ice cold drink in the summertime.
And if I don't manage to wake up at dawn every day and work,
work!—then promise me you'll desert me forever, Ivan Romanych.

CHEBUTYKIN

(Tenderly) I promise to desert you forever.

OLGA

Father had us up at seven. Now Irina opens her *eyes* at seven but
she lies in bed until nine, thinking, thinking. With such a serious
look on her face. *(Laughs)*

IRINA

You look at me like a little girl, so you think it's strange if my face
looks serious, but I'm all grown up!

TUZENBACH

Work, God, yes. I never worked a day in my life. I was born in
Petersburg, where it's cold and people are lazy. And my family
never knew hardship. I remember when I got home from school,
our servant would take off my boots while I threw a tantrum. But

my mother just looked at me adoringly, surprised if the servants looked less than adoring as I kicked them. My parents kept me from hard work, always.

But now times have changed, there's a hurricane on the horizon, gathering speed and force, and soon it will be here! A great and terrible wind will clean out our lazy, sick indifference, and anyone who has ever expressed boredom will be washed clean out. I myself will work, and in twenty-five or thirty years we will all work! Everyone.

CHEBUTYKIN

Not me.

TUZENBACH

You don't count.

SOLYONY

You won't be alive in twenty-five years, thank God. In a few years you'll have a heart attack and drop dead, my friend; or else I'll lose my temper, and put a bullet through your head.

Solyony rubs perfume on his hands and chest.
Chebutykin laughs.

CHEBUTYKIN

I've never done a thing. After I left school, I didn't lift a finger, never got to the end of a book. I read the newspaper.

Takes out another newspaper.

CHEBUTYKIN

And I read in the paper about some famous writer, so now I know his name, and the fact that he's famous, but what he says, I have no idea.

A knock, people banging from below.

21

CHEBUTYKIN

Ah! It's for me, a visitor, I'll be right there . . .

He exits.

IRINA

He's got something up his sleeve.

TUZENBACH

Indeed, he looked rather triumphant. He must have a large present for you.

IRINA

Oh, how unpleasant!

OLGA

Oh, yes, it's awful. He can be such a little boy.

MASHA

By the bending sea, a green oak tree,
Where a golden chain is bound—

OLGA

You're not happy, Masha.

Masha, whistling, puts on a hat.

OLGA

Where are you going?

MASHA

Home.

IRINA

That's strange.

TUZENBACH

You'd leave a birthday!

MASHA

Oh, it's all the same day. I'll come back tonight. Bye, darling. *(Kisses Irina)* I wish you health and happiness. Back when Father was alive, thirty or forty officers would come to our parties, and it was wonderfully loud. But today we have approximately one and a half men and it's about as loud as the desert. I'm leaving. A touch of melancholy, as they say. I'm no fun right now; don't listen to me.

Laughing through tears.

We can have a good talk later, but good-bye for now, darling, I'm off. I'll go—somewhere.

IRINA

(Vexed) You're really something.

OLGA

(Through tears) I understand you, Masha.

SOLYONY

When a man talks philosophy you get sophistry but when a woman talks philosophy, or God forbid two, you might as well pull my finger. *(He makes a farting sound and laughs)*

MASHA

What's that supposed to mean, you horrible man?

SOLYONY

Oh, nothing.
A man cannot breathe in any case
When a brown bear comes and sits on his face.
And that—is how life is.

MASHA

(To Olga) Oh, stop blubbering!

Enter Anfisa and Ferapont, with a birthday cake.

ANFISA

Come in, come in, old man, your feet are clean—A cake! From
Protopopov at the council office.

IRINA

Thanks. Tell him I said thanks.

FERAPONT

What?

IRINA

(Shouting) Thank him!

OLGA

Nanny, get Ferapont some cake.
(To Ferapont) Ferapont, go, get yourself some cake.

FERAPONT

What?

ANFISA

Come with me, Grandpa, let's go.

MASHA

I don't like Protopop—Popov—whatever his name is, you
shouldn't have invited him.

IRINA

I didn't.

MASHA

Good.

*Chebutykin comes in carrying a huge silver tea service. Murmurs of
surprise and displeasure.*

OLGA

(Her face in her hands) A samovar! My, God! That's for a husband
to give a wife! How awful.

She exits.
The below three lines, simultaneously:

IRINA	TUZENBACH	MASHA
(To Chebutykin) Ivan Romanich, why?	Told you so.	Ivan Romanich, you should be ashamed of yourself.

CHEBUTYKIN

My dears, my darlings, you're all I've got, I love you more than anything in the world. I'm an old man, a husk of a man, aware of my own insignificance . . . The best thing about me is my love for you, and if it weren't for you three, I'd have given up the ghost long ago. *(To Irina)* Darling, I've known you since the day you were born . . . I held you in my arms . . . I loved your mother, may she rest in peace . . .

IRINA

But why such expensive presents!

CHEBUTYKIN

Expensive presents! That's ridiculous . . . *(To a soldier)* Put the samovar over there. *(Mimicking her)* Expensive presents . . .

Anfisa enters.

ANFISA

My dears, a strange colonel, at the door. A stranger, never seen him before. Already took his overcoat off, my angels, he's on his way in. *(To Irina)* Iri, be nice. Our lunch is already getting cold. Lord have mercy!

TUZENBACH

Must be Vershinin.

Enter Vershinin.

TUZENBACH

Lieutenant Colonel Vershinin!

VERSHININ

I have the honor of presenting myself.
Vershinin.

He salutes, military style.

VERSHININ

I'm so happy to finally be in your home.
(To Irina and Masha) Ay, look at you! What you've become!

IRINA

Sit anywhere. We're so glad you've come.

VERSHININ

Happy I'm here, happy I'm here! But you are three sisters.
I remember—three girls. I don't remember your faces, but
I remember that your father, Colonel Prozorov, had three little
girls. I saw you with my own eyes. Ah, ah! *(Some American equivalent of Ay, ay, ach, oy, oy, etc.)* How time flies. How time flies . . .

TUZENBACH

He's from Moscow.

IRINA

Moscow! You're from Moscow!

VERSHININ

Yes. Your father was a commander in Moscow, and I was an officer under his command. *(To Masha)* Now, *your* face I believe
I remember.

MASHA

But I you? No.

IRINA

Olya, Olya! *(Calling with childlike excitement to the dining room)*
Olya! Come quick.

Olga enters.

IRINA

Colonel Vershinin—from Moscow!

VERSHININ

You must be Olga, the oldest. And you're Masha, and you're Irina, the baby—

OLGA

You're from Moscow?

VERSHININ

Yes. I studied in Moscow and joined the army there, served for a long time, and finally got my own command—here—in this town. Funny, I don't really remember you, but I remember that there were three sisters.

Your father remains perfectly stamped in my memory. If I close my eyes I can still see him under my eyelids. I used to go to your house in Moscow—

OLGA

I thought I remembered everyone, but—now—

VERSHININ

My full name is: Aleksandr Ignatyevich.

IRINA

Alexander Ignatyevich, from Moscow! What a surprise!

OLGA

We're moving back, in fact.

IRINA

Perhaps by September. It's *our city*!
(*Endow "our city" with the meaning—our native land, motherland, that which pulls you*)
We were *born* there . . . On Old Basmanny Street . . .

Olga and Irina laugh with joy.

27

MASHA

(Deadpan, as though to say: my sisters think of Moscow as a country) Oh, a fellow countryman.

(Suddenly very alive) Oh, now I remember! I do! Olya—do you remember—they used to tell stories about the "Lovesick Major?" You were a low-ranking soldier then, but you were in love, so they teased you and called you: "The lovesick major."

VERSHININ

Yes, that's it! "The lovesick major," that was me.

MASHA

You only had little whiskers then . . . Oh, you're older now! *(Through tears)* You're old!

VERSHININ

Yes, they used to call me the lovesick major, because I was young and I was in love. Now—times have changed.

OLGA

But you don't have a single gray hair. You're older but you're not *old*.

VERSHININ

And yet, I'm forty-three. When did you come from Moscow?

IRINA

Eleven years ago. Masha, what's wrong? Don't cry, silly, you'll make me cry. *(Almost in tears)*

MASHA

I—nothing.
What street did you live on?

VERSHININ

Old Basmanny!

OLGA

Same as us!

VERSHININ

And then I lived on Nemesky Street. I'd walk on Nemesky Street down to the barracks—remember that sad old bridge down there? Water rushing under your feet—what a sound! Alone on that bridge, the sound could make your soul go all cold.

Pause.

But this river—here—is such a joyful, big river! Wide, and strong!

OLGA

Yes, but cold. Cold with mosquitoes.

VERSHININ

Oh, come on now, it's good weather here—fresh, bracing, healthy—Slavic! A forest, a river, and—birch trees. Birches, as humble as they are beautiful. Of all trees, I love them best. It's a good life here. But strange, no train station for eighteen miles. And no one knows why.

SOLYONY

I know why.

They all stare at him.

SOLYONY

Because if the station were near, then it wouldn't be far, and if it were far, it wouldn't be near.

An odd silence.

TUZENBACH

Ha ha ha, Vassily Vassilich.

OLGA

(To Vershinin) Now I remember you. I remember.

VERSHININ

I knew your mother.

CHEBUTYKIN

A good woman, God bless her soul.

IRINA

Mama is buried in Moscow.

OLGA

In Novodevichy cemetery.

MASHA

Imagine, I'm already beginning to forget her face.
One day no one will remember us either. We'll be forgotten too.

VERSHININ

True. We'll be forgotten. That's life, there's no getting around it.
Our projects, our obsessions—serious, big, important—a time
will come when they won't be important anymore.

Pause.

And you can't guess what will be considered vast and important,
and what will be considered small and ridiculous. When Columbus and Copernicus first appeared, people thought they were
laughable, while some backwards drivel written by an idiot was
the Gospel truth!

And it may be that our lives, so familiar and dear to us, will in
time seem strange, stupid, disgusting, or even depraved.

TUZENBACH

Who knows? They might call us stewards of knowledge, a high
point of civilization. We don't have torture, capital punishment,
invasions—but still . . . all the suffering . . .

SOLYONY

(Makes high-pitched chicken sounds for feeding chickens) Cheep
cheep cheep . . .
You don't need chicken seed for the Baron,
he can dine upon philosophy.

TUZENBACH

Will you leave me alone for God's sake? Your jokes are getting
boring.

SOLYONY

(Higher voice) Cheep cheep cheep!

TUZENBACH

But in spite of all the suffering, there are other cultural improve-
ments, moral progress—

VERSHININ

Yes, yes, of course.

CHEBUTYKIN

You said, Baron, they'll call our lives a high point, but people
are basically low. *(Stands up)* Look how short I am, for instance.
Keep calling me elevated, I like it.

A violin is heard offstage.

MASHA

That's Andrei playing, our brother.

IRINA

He's the scholar of the family. He was born to be a professor.
Father was a military man, but he gave birth to an academic.

MASHA

That's what Papa wanted for him.

OLGA

I'm afraid we teased him today. He's in love.

IRINA

With a local girl. She might come to lunch.

MASHA

Oh, and her clothes! They're not ugly or unfashionable, they're just sad. A strange loud yellowish skirt with a pathetic fringe— topped off with a red jacket. And her pink cheeks, scrubbed, scrubbed, scrubbed until they're like apples! Andrei can't be in love, I won't allow it. He's got some taste, he's just teasing us. I heard she's marrying Protopopov, chairman of the county council, which would be perfect. Andrei, come here! Just for a minute, dear!

The violin stops. Enter Andrei.

OLGA

This is my brother, Andrei.

VERSHININ

Vershinin.

ANDREI

Nice to meet you. *(Wipes his face)* You're the new battery commander?

OLGA

He's from Moscow!

ANDREI

Oh? Well, congratulations, now my sisters won't leave you alone.

VERSHININ

I think I've already bored your sisters.

IRINA

Look at this picture frame Andrei gave me today for my birthday! He made it himself.

Pulling it out.

VERSHININ

(Looking at frame and not knowing what to say) Oh—yes—what
a thing—

IRINA

And this one on the piano, he made that too.

Andrei waves his hand and moves away.

OLGA

Andrei's our little scholar; he plays the violin and can carve so
many many objects out of wood. He's practically a Renaissance
man. Andrei, don't go! He's always wandering off. Come back!

They lead him back, laughing.

MASHA

Come on, come on!

ANDREI

Leave me alone—

MASHA

You're being silly! Vershinin used to be called the lovesick major,
and he didn't get upset.

VERSHININ

Not in the least!

MASHA

I'll call you—the lovesick violinist!

IRINA

Or the lovesick professor!

OLGA

Andrei's in love! Andryusha's in love!

IRINA

Bravo, bravo! Andryusha's in love!

CHEBUTYKIN

(Approaching Andrei from behind, taking him by the waist with both arms and singing) For love, sweet love alone, did Nature put us on this earth to roam . . . *(Laughing)*

ANDREI

Enough, enough already. I didn't sleep at all last night, and I'm not myself today. *(Wiping his face)* I stayed up reading until four, then I went to bed, but nothing happened. I thought of this and that, and suddenly the sun is climbing into my bedroom, so early. This summer, while I'm here, I want to translate this wonderful English novel—

VERSHININ

You read English?

ANDREI

Yes. Father, may he rest in peace, oppressed us with education. He really cracked the whip. I know it sounds funny, but after he died, I started to put on the pounds. It was like my body was suddenly freeing itself of my father and his discipline. Thanks to my father, we all know French, German, English, and Irina knows *Italiano*. But at what cost!

MASHA

It's a silly affectation to know three languages in a town like this one. No—not even an affectation—it's an extra appendage. Like having a sixth finger. We know too much.

VERSHININ

(Laughing) Oh, you know too much! How can that be, I can't believe any town could be so backward that it has no place for intelligent, educated people. Imagine that out of one hundred thousand people in this town—I agree, it's a little forlorn—and lacks culture—okay—but let's say there are only three people like

you three sisters. Of course, you can't transform the masses—
you will instead dissolve *into* them—you will be silenced, by life,
life itself will hush you up, but you won't dissolve without an
imprint. After your death there will be six more like you, then
twelve, and so on, and so on, until people like you—enlight-
ened people—will become the majority! In two or three hundred
years, life on earth will be beyond beautiful, beyond imagination,
sublime—man *needs* that life, and if it doesn't yet exist, he must
sense it coming—wait for it—prepare for it by dreaming of it!
And that is why we must perceive more deeply than our parents
perceived, see more fully than our grandparents saw.

(Laughing) And you complain that you know too much!

MASHA

I'll stay for lunch.

She takes off her hat.

IRINA

(Sighing) You should write that all down . . .

Andrei exits.
No one notices.

TUZENBACH

You say that life on earth will be beautiful, sublime. Could be. But
to experience even a fraction of that beauty, even now, from far
off, we need to lay the groundwork, we need to work—

VERSHININ

Yes. *(Rises)* Look at all these flowers! *(Looks around)*
What a beautiful place you all live in! I'm jealous. I've lived my
life in tiny apartments with two chairs, a couch, and heaters that
sputter. I think what I've been missing all my life—are exactly
these flowers.

(Throws his hands up) Ah, well. What can you do.

TUZENBACH

Yes. We need to work. You might think: there's the German, getting sentimental. But, look, I'm Russian. I don't even speak German. My father was Russian Orthodox . . .

Pause.

VERSHININ

(Pacing) I often think: what if we could begin life over again, consciously? The life we'd lived before would be a smudgy rough draft, and the new life would be clean—the book itself! Then we wouldn't repeat our old mistakes, we'd at least invent for ourselves a new setting: a room full of flowers and masses of light! I have a wife and two little girls, and my wife is not a—well lady, and so on. But if I started my life over again from the very beginning—I wouldn't be married. No, no.

Enter Kulygin, wearing a high school teacher's uniform.

KULYGIN

(To Irina) My dear sister-in-law, allow me to congratulate you on the day of your birthday and to wish you sincerely from my heart, health and everything else a girl your age might wish, within the bounds of reason and propriety. Here is a token, from me to you, a history of our local high school, written by yours truly. It's a little nothing, a trifle, I wrote it long ago, when I had nothing better to do, but all the same, read it. Good afternoon, everyone! *(To Vershinin)* The name's Kulygin, teacher at the local high school, civil servant of the seventh class. *(To Irina)* You can find every single graduate of our high school in this little book, every name for the past fifty years. Feci quod potui, faciant meliora potentes. *(Kisses Masha)*

IRINA

You gave me this book last Easter.

KULYGIN

(Laughing) No! Did I? All right then, give it back! Or let's give it to the colonel. Here, Colonel. Read it when you're overcome with boredom.

VERSHININ

(Bowing) Thank you. *(Leaving)* I'm overjoyed that I met all of you.

OLGA

You're leaving? No, don't!

IRINA

Stay for lunch. Please do.

OLGA

We insist.

VERSHININ

I seem to have barged in on a birthday party. I'm so sorry, I had no idea! I would have said happy birthday . . .

He exits with Olga.

KULYGIN

Today, ladies and gentleman, is Sunday. The day of rest. And so let us rest, each according to his age and capacity. The rugs need to be rolled up for the summer, hiding until winter—in mothballs . . . The Romans were a robust people—they knew how to work hard and how to rest—mens sana in corpore sano. Their lives moved in regular orbit, pattern and form. Our headmaster says the most important thing in life is form—when things lose their form, they lose their nature. And the same is true of everyday life. *(Puts his arm around Masha, laughing)*

Masha loves me. My wife loves me. And the curtains should go with the rugs. Today I'm happy, in fine fiddle. Masha, we're expected at the headmaster's at four o'clock. They've arranged a little hike for faculty, and for faculty wives.

MASHA

I'm not going.

KULYGIN

(Grief-stricken) Masha my Masha-mine, why not?

MASHA

(Angry) We'll talk later.
Fine, I'll go, but please—leave me alone . . . *(She exits)*

KULYGIN

So we'll spend the evening with the headmaster. In spite of his
weak constitution, he does his best to be social. A shining exam-
ple to us all. A magnificent, magnanimous man!
Yesterday, after the faculty meeting, he says to me, "I'm tired,
Fyodor, exhausted."
(Looks at clock) Your clock is seven minutes fast.
"Yes," he says, "I'm exhausted."

A violin offstage.

OLGA

(Entering) Ladies and gentlemen, come and eat! We have pie!

KULYGIN

Ach, dear Olga, my dear, yesterday I worked from dawn until
eleven o'clock and I was so tired, but today I'm happy. *(Goes to
the table)* . . . My dear.

CHEBUTYKIN

(Combing out his beard) Pie! Magnificent!

MASHA

(Sternly to Chebutykin) But not a drop of liquor for you, hear me?
It's bad for you.

CHEBUTYKIN

Oh, blah blah blah. That's over and done with. I haven't been
blotto in two years. And who gives a damn if I am!

MASHA

I do, so don't drink, don't dare, period.
(So her husband can't hear) Goddamnit, another boring night at
the headmaster's.

TUZENBACH

If I were you, I wouldn't go. Simple as that.

CHEBUTYKIN

Don't go, my darling . . .

MASHA

Don't go my darling, easy for you to say . . .
what a miserable goddamn life.

CHEBUTYKIN

Now, now . . .

Everyone but Irina and Tuzenbach goes to the dining room.

SOLYONY

(Crossing to the dining room) Cheep cheep cheep.

TUZENBACH

That's enough, Vasily Vasilych. That will do.

SOLYONY

Here, chickee, chickee—

KULYGIN

(Cheerfully) To your health, Colonel! I'm a teacher by profession,
but here I'm sort of my own man. And Masha's husband. She's a
good one, you know, she's a good woman.

VERSHININ

I'll have some vodka. *(Drinks)* Cheers! To your health! *(To Olga)*
I feel as if I've come home.

Irina and Tuzenbach in the living room.

IRINA

Masha isn't herself today. She married at eighteen, when she
thought her husband the most intelligent man. Not now. He's the
most good, but not the most intelligent.

OLGA

Andrei! Come on, finally!

ANDREI

(Entering) Now!

In a private corner of the living room.

TUZENBACH

What are you thinking?

IRINA

It's just . . . I don't like that friend of yours, Solyony. He scares me. Everything that comes out of his mouth is nonsense.

TUZENBACH

He's a strange duck. I feel bad for him and he grates on me, but mostly I feel bad for him. I think he's probably shy. When it's only me and him, he can be very smart and even sweet, but in a group, he's rude, a bully.

Don't go yet, let them unfold their napkins. Let me be around you. What are you thinking?

Pause.

You're young . . . Think how many years we have ahead of us! A long long carpet of days, unfolding, full of my love for you . . .

IRINA

Oh, don't talk to me about love.

TUZENBACH

(Not listening)
I want to live Irina, I have this hunger for struggle, for labor, and this hunger merges in my soul with my love for you, Irina . . . as if by design: you are so beautiful, and for that reason, life seems to me just as beautiful. What are you thinking?

IRINA

You say: life is beautiful.
But what if it only seems that way.
For us, three sisters, life has not been beautiful—
it chokes us, like weeds.
Oh, tears— *(She starts crying)*
are not necessary—

Quickly wipes her face and smiles.

IRINA

Work. We need to work.
That's why we're unhappy—we stare at life from the outside in,
through a dark pane of glass, thinking it awful,
because we don't know how to work.
We were born to parents who despised labor.

Natasha enters, wearing a pink dress with a green belt.

NATASHA

Oh, they're eating already . . . oh, dear, I'm late. *(She primps in the mirror)* The hair is not so bad . . . *(Seeing Irina)* My dear Irina Sergeyevna, happy birthday! *(Kisses her on both cheeks strong and long, three times)* So many guests! I feel quite shy. *Hello,* Baron!

OLGA

(Entering living room) Ah, Natalya Ivanovna has arrived. Hello, my *dear* girl.

They kiss.

NATASHA

It's such a big fancy party, I had no idea, I'm terribly shy.

OLGA

Don't be silly, we're all old friends. *(Under her breath)* You're wearing a green belt! My dear, that's not good!

41

NATASHA

Why? Is it bad luck?

OLGA

No, it just doesn't suit your dress. It's somehow strange.

NATASHA
(Quivering voice)
Do you think so? It's not really *green*-green though, it's more of a greeny-beige . . .

She follows them into the dining room.

KULYGIN

I hope you find yourself a good husband, Irina. Your clock is ticking.

CHEBUTYKIN

Natalya, I hope you catch a husband too.

KULYGIN

Natalya already has a fiancé.

MASHA
(Striking her fork against her plate) Another glass of wine for me! What the hell, life is a raspberry—one little bite and it's gone!

KULYGIN

You get a C minus for behavior.

VERSHININ

This vodka is delicious. What's in it?

SOLYONY

Cockroaches.

IRINA

Oh! Why do you have to be so disgusting?

OLGA

For dinner, we'll be roasting a bird and having pie. I'm home all day, thank God, and this evening, so I hope all of you can join us again for dinner.

VERSHININ

Will you allow me the honor of coming?

IRINA

Of course.

NATASHA

They don't stand on ceremony here.

CHEBUTYKIN

(Singing) For love, sweet love alone, did Nature put us on this earth to roam . . . *(He laughs)*

ANDREI

Oh, stop it! Aren't you sick of yourselves?

Fedotik and Rodé enter with a big basket of flowers.

FEDOTIK

They're already eating lunch.

RODÉ

(Loudly and affected) Dining? Yes they're dining!

FEDOTIK

Hold still! *(Takes a photograph)*
One more! Wait a minute!
(Takes another. They are all frozen, for a long moment)
Now you can all move again.

RODÉ

(Loud) Happy birthday! I wish you everything, everything! It's beautiful out today, shockingly beautiful. I walked all morning with my students. I teach gym at the high school . . .

FEDOTIK

You can move, Irina, you can move now.
(Taking picture, looking at her) You are interesting today.
(Takes a top out of his pocket) Look what I brought, it makes this crazy sound.

IRINA

It's delightful!

MASHA

By the bending sea, a green oak tree,
Where a golden chain is bound—
And on that chain a cultured cat
spins round and round and round—

Why am I saying this? This phrase stuck in me since early morning . . .

KULYGIN

There are now thirteen of us!

RODÉ

(Loudly) Ladies and gentlemen, you're not superstitious, are you?

Laughter.

KULYGIN

When thirteen people sit down to eat, it means two of them are in love. Is it you, Ivan Romanovich? God help us!

Laughter.

CHEBUTYKIN

I'm an old sinner, but why is Natalya Ivanovna blushing? I can't imagine . . .

More laughter. Natasha runs to the living room, Andrei follows.

ANDREI

It's all right, don't listen to them! Wait. Wait a minute, please . . .

NATASHA

I'm so embarrassed. I don't know what's happening inside me—
they always laugh at me. I know it's terrible manners to leave the
table like that, but I can't, I can't . . .

Covers face with hands.

ANDREI

My darling, please, don't take it to heart. Trust me, they're jok-
ing, they mean well. My darling, they're sincere, good people,
they love me, and you.

He draws her to an unseen window.

NATASHA

I'm just not used to high society.

ANDREI

Oh, youth! Beautiful, perfect youth!
Darling, my love, don't worry! Believe me, believe me, it feels
so pure, so good, so alive! I'm happy, my soul is giddy with love!
With ecstasy! What is it, what, made me fall in love with you, and
why? I have no idea! My dear good, my pure darling, be my wife.
I love you, love, like no one! Never!

They kiss.
Two officers enter, shocked to see them kissing.

Act II

Same setting. Eight o'clock. No lights.
The sound of an accordian, from far off.
Natasha enters with a candle and stops in front of Andrei's room.

NATASHA

What are you doing, Andryusha—reading? Oh, it's nothing . . .
(Goes to another door, opens it, looks in) No lamps lit—

ANDREI

(Entering with a book in his hand) Natasha? What is it?

NATASHA

Just wanted to make sure no lamps are burning. During the holidays, the help forgets absolutely everything. You have to watch them like a hawk or the house will simply fall to pieces. Last night at twelve o'clock I saw a candle burning in the living room! I still don't know who left it burning. *(Puts candle down)* What time is it?

ANDREI

After eight.

NATASHA

And Olga and Irina still working. Always working, poor things.
Olga's at some teacher's meeting, Irina's at the telegraph office.
(Sighs) This morning I said to your sister, I said, "You really
must save your strength, Irina, my dove." But she didn't listen.
Eight-fifteen, you said? I'm worried our little Bobik is sick. Why
is he so cold? Yesterday he was so hot, now he's so cold, I'm worried sick.

ANDREI

He's fine, Natasha, he's healthy.

NATASHA

Maybe. But I think I'll start him on a new diet. I'm afraid! And the
carolers are descending on us tonight—it's better if they don't
come, Andrusha.

ANDREI

I don't know. They were invited.

NATASHA

This morning the baby woke up and looked at me, and he smiled
this beautiful smile. And I knew that he recognized me! "Bobik!"
I said, "Bobilicious! Hello, my little boy." And he laughed!
Babies are so smart, they understand absolutely everything. So—
Andrusha—I'll tell the servants *not* to let the carolers in tonight.

ANDREI

(Unsure) But it's up to my sisters. They're in charge.

NATASHA

Of course, they're in charge, too. I'll tell them what I decided.
They're so sweet. *(Leaving)* I've ordered yogurt for dinner. The
doctor says you need to eat yogurt, and only yogurt, or you won't
lose any weight. *(Stops)* Bobik's cold, I'm afraid he's cold in that
room. He *must* be cold. We should move him to another room, at
least until it's warmer. Irina's room, for instance, would be perfect for a baby! It's dry and gets sun all day. I'll tell her she can

share a room with Olga. She won't care, she's hardly home. She only sleeps here.

Pause.

Sweetie, sweetie-pie. Why are you so quiet?

ANDREI
Just lost in thought. What is there to say?

NATASHA
True enough. Now there was something else I wanted to tell you. Oh, right, Ferapont is here from the council. He wants to talk to you.

ANDREI
(Yawning) Send him in.

Natasha exits.
Andrei reads his book, leaning in toward the candle Natasha forgot.
Ferapont enters, wearing an old coat and a scarf around his ears.

ANDREI
Hello, old friend. What can you tell me?

FERAPONT
The Chairman sent you a book and some papers. Here.

Gives him the books and papers.

ANDREI
Thanks. Good. But why didn't you come earlier? It's almost nine o'clock.

FERAPONT
What?

ANDREI
(Loud) I said, why so late? It's almost nine!

49

FERAPONT

True enough, sir. It was still light out when I came to find you, but they wouldn't let me in. "The master's busy," they said. Okay, if you're busy, you're busy, I thought. I'm in no hurry. *(Thinks Andrei said something)* What?

ANDREI

Nothing. *(Looks through the book)*
Tomorrow's Friday, there are no meetings, but I'll stop in anyway. Keep busy. It's boring at home.

Pause.

Oh, my friend, life is so strangely changing, so deceptive! Today I was bored so I picked up this book—my old notes from university—and I thought, how absurd! My God, I'm a clerk for the county council, lorded over by Protopopov. I'm a clerk, the most I could hope for is to become a full member of a provincial county council. Me!—on the county council—me, the same man who dreams every night he's a professor at Moscow University, a public intellectual, the pride of Russia!

FERAPONT

Dunno . . . my hearing's bad . . .

ANDREI

If you could hear, I probably wouldn't talk to you.
I need to talk to someone. My wife doesn't understand me; my sisters I'm afraid of, I don't know why. I'm afraid they'll poke fun at me, humiliate me.
I don't drink, I don't like bars, but how happy I'd be in Moscow right this minute, sitting on a stool at Testev's, or the Grand Moscow.

FERAPONT

Speaking of Moscow, a guy at the office was telling a story the other day. Some guys in Moscow, businessmen, were eating blintzes. One of them ate forty blintzes—dropped dead. Maybe it was forty, maybe fifty. Can't remember.

ANDREI

In Moscow you can be sitting in a huge restaurant full of people. You don't know anyone and no one knows you, but you don't feel like a stranger. Here, in this town, you know everyone, and everyone knows you, but you feel like a foreigner. A stranger. Strange, and alone.

FERAPONT

What?

Pause.

FERAPONT

Oh, and this same guy was saying—now he could have been making this up—there's this rope, he says, stretches all the way across Moscow.

ANDREI

What for?

FERAPONT

Dunno. That's what the guy said.

ANDREI

He made it up. *(Reading his book)*
Have you ever been to Moscow?

FERAPONT

Nope. Not in God's plan.

Pause.

Mind if I go?

ANDREI

Yes, go then. Good night.

Ferapont exits, Andrei's nose is still in his book.

ANDREI

Good night. You can pick up these papers tomorrow morning.
Go ahead, now.

Pause.

He's gone.

A doorbell rings.

ANDREI

Oh, well.

He stretches and goes to his room.
Offstage the nurse sings a lullaby to the baby.
Masha and Vershinin enter the living room, talking.
As they talk, a maid lights the lamps.

MASHA

I don't know.

I don't know. Of course, you can get used to anything. It took
us a while after Father died to get used to not having all of his
officers around the house. It may be different in other towns, but
here, the most well-mannered, cultured, attractive people are in
the military!

VERSHININ

I'm suddenly thirsty. I'd love some tea.

MASHA

(Looking at the clock) It'll be ready soon. They married me off
when I was eighteen. I was afraid of my husband because he was
a teacher and I was barely out of school. I thought he was the
most wise, cultured, important man I'd ever met. Not anymore.
Oh well.

VERSHININ

Well . . . yes.

MASHA

And the rest of the people in this town—and I don't mean my husband, I'm used to him—they're so rude, they have no manners, no culture. I get so upset when people are stupid, rude, unthinking—I actually suffer when I see someone with no manners, with no gentleness. When I'm forced to spend time with my husband's colleagues, I suffer.

VERSHININ

Yes . . . but it seems to me, the military and civilians are equally uninteresting. At least in this town, it's all the same. Listen to any soldier or intellectual around here—he's sick of his wife, he's sick of his house, he's sick of his horse. Russians are supposed to be lofty thinkers—right? Our heads are in the clouds—but our feet are in the mud. In life, why do we reach so low? Why?

MASHA

Why?

VERSHININ

Why are we sick of our children, sick of our wives? Why are they sick and tired of us?

MASHA

You're not yourself today.

VERSHININ

Could be. I forgot to eat lunch. I haven't eaten since morning. And my daughter's under the weather. My conscience eats away at me when my daughters are sick—it kills me, what they've got for a mother. You should have seen her today, she's almost not a person. We started fighting at seven this morning, and I slammed the door at nine. And left.

Pause.

I never talk about this. It's strange, you're the only one I complain to . . .

53

He kisses her hand.

Don't be angry with me. Without you, I have no one, no one . . .

Pause.

MASHA

What a strange sound in the chimney. Before my father died, the chimney made a whooshing noise, just like that.

VERSHININ

Are you superstitious?

MASHA

Yes.

VERSHININ

Funny. *(Kisses her hand)* You are a wondrous, magnificent woman. Magnificent-wondrous! It's dark but I can see your eyes, how they shine.

MASHA

(Moving to another chair) There's more light here.

VERSHININ

I love, love, love . . . love your eyes, and I dream of how you move . . . Magnificent, wondrous woman.

MASHA

(Laughing quietly) When you talk that way, I laugh, even though I'm afraid.
Don't speak, I beg you . . . *(Under her breath)*
Oh, keep talking. What the hell . . . *(Covers her face with her hands)*
Someone's coming, change the subject.

Irina and Tuzenbach enter.

TUZENBACH

I have three last names. They call me: Baron Tuzenbach-Krone-Altschauer. But I'm really Russian Orthodox, like you. I've retained only my German stubbornness and my patience. I will wear you out with patience. I walk you home every night.

IRINA

I'm so tired!

TUZENBACH

And I'll continue to walk you home every night from that telegraph office, for the next ten to twenty years, unless you shoo me away. *(Happy to see Masha and Vershinin)* Oh it's you! Hello!

IRINA

Oh, God, I'm finally home. *(To Masha)* Today a woman needed to telegraph her brother that her son died. And she can't for the life of her remember his address. So she sends it without an address, just writes down a name, and a town. She was crying. I was rude to her for no reason. I said: "I don't have time for this." It just came out. Oh, how stupid! Are the carolers coming tonight?

MASHA

Yes.

IRINA

(Sitting down) I have to rest. I'm tired.

TUZENBACH

When you come home from work, you look like a sad child . . .

IRINA

I'm tired. I hate the telegraph office, I really do.

MASHA

You look thinner . . . *(Whistles)* . . . younger—your face is starting to look like a boy's.

TUZENBACH
Because of her hairstyle.

IRINA
I have to find another job. This one doesn't suit me, not at all. The things I wanted, the things I dreamed of—are not at the telegraph office. It's labor, without poetry, without meaning.

A knock from the floor below.

IRINA
The doctor's knocking. *(To Tuzenbach)* Would you knock back, dear? I can't . . . too tired . . .

Tuzenbach knocks on the floor.

IRINA
He's coming now. We need to do something. Last night the doctor and Andrei were out at the club gambling again. They say Andrei lost two hundred roubles.

MASHA
(Indifferently) What can we do now . . .

IRINA
He lost in December, then he lost again two weeks ago. If he'd just go ahead and lose everything, maybe we could leave this town. Oh, God! I dream of Moscow every night. I'm like a crazy person. *(Laughs)* We move in June, so—January, February, March, April, May—that's almost half a year!

MASHA
We can't let Natasha find out about all the money he's lost.

IRINA
I can't imagine that she cares.

Chebutykin enters, combing his beard, just up from a nap. He sits at the dining room table and takes out a newspaper.

MASHA

Here he is. Has he paid rent?

IRINA

No, not for the last eight months, he's clearly forgotten.

MASHA

(Laughing) Look at him sitting like that!

Everybody laughs. Pause.

IRINA

(To Vershinin) Why are you so quiet?

VERSHININ

I don't know. I'd like some tea. Half my life for a cup of tea! I forgot to eat this morning . . .

CHEBUTYKIN

Irina Sergeyevna!

IRINA

What is it?

CHEBUTYKIN

Come here. Venez ici.

Irina goes to him.

CHEBUTYKIN

I'm lost without you.

She lays out a card game.

VERSHININ

Well, if the tea isn't coming, we might as well philosophize.

TUZENBACH

Let's. About what?

VERSHININ

About what. We could dream a little . . . For instance, life as it will be lived after we're gone, in two or three hundred years.

TUZENBACH

Well, after we're gone, people will most likely fly in balloons, wear a different cut of coat and discover a sixth sense.
But life will essentially be just the same.
It's difficult, and happy, and full of mystery.
A thousand years from now, people will still be sighing, just as we do: Oh, life is hard!
All the same, they will fear death. And try to avoid dying.
Just as we do now.

VERSHININ

(After a moment's thought) How can I say this? I think everything in the world changes, little moment by little moment, while we're watching life go by, it's changing, imperceptibly. In two or three hundred years—or a thousand—a new life, a happy life, will begin, and we won't be part of it, but it's what we live for, now. We're working—we're *suffering*—for it, without realizing it, we're *building* it. And that's the purpose of our being here at all; you might say: that alone *is our happiness.*

Masha laughs.

TUZENBACH

What's funny?

MASHA

I don't know. I started laughing this morning and now I can't stop laughing.

VERSHININ

I went to the same school as you did but I didn't make it to college. I read a lot—never learned how to choose the right books, maybe I haven't read the right books, but the more I live, the

more I want to know. My hair is turning gray—any minute now I'll be an old man—and still I know so little, so very little. But the one important, real thing I *do* know (and I know it well) I only wish I could prove it to you:
Happiness isn't ours to have, nor should it be.
All we can do is work, and work, and work,
and if any happiness comes of it, we'll leave it for those who come long after us.

Not for me, but for my own ones, and for theirs, who come after.

Fedotik and Rodé play the guitar.

TUZENBACH

According to you, we shouldn't even dream of happiness! But what if I'm happy?

VERSHININ

No.

TUZENBACH

(Throwing up his hands and laughing) Obviously we don't see eye to eye. How can I convince you? *(Masha laughs. He wags a finger at her)* Okay, laugh! *(To Vershinin)* Two or three hundred years, it's immaterial. Even in a million years, life will be exactly the same. Life is unchanging, remains constant, follows its own laws—laws that aren't any of our business, that we'll never understand.
Birds who migrate—cranes—they fly on and on—no matter what thoughts, big or small, wander into their heads.
They fly, not knowing why or where.
Even if one or two birds become a philosopher, still they fly.
It doesn't matter what a couple of them philosophizes,
as long as they all keep flying together.

MASHA

But there must be meaning.

TUZENBACH

Meaning . . . Look: it's snowing. What is the meaning of snow?

Pause.

MASHA

I think a person has to believe in something,
or search out some kind of faith;
otherwise life is empty, nothing.
How can you live not knowing why the cranes fly,
why children are born, why there are stars in the sky . . .
Either you know why you live,
or it's all small, unnecessary bits.

Pause.

VERSHININ

Too bad we can't stay young.

MASHA

Gogol wrote: Ladies and gentleman, life is boring!

TUZENBACH

And I say, ladies and gentlemen, you're impossible to argue with!
You're completely—

CHEBUTYKIN

(Reading the newspaper) Balzac was married in Berdichev.

Irinia sings or hums quietly.

CHEBUTYKIN

I must write that down in my little book. Balzac was married in
Berdichev.

Reads newspaper.

IRINA

(Laying out a game of cards)
Balzac was married in Berdichev.

TUZENBACH

The die is cast. Maria Sergeyevna, I'm resigning from the military.

MASHA

I heard. Too bad. I hate civilians.

TUZENBACH

Ah, who cares. *(Gets up)* I'm ugly—so what kind of military figure can I cut? Oh, who cares. But I'm going to start working. For once I want to work so hard that when I come home at night, dead tired, I can pour myself into bed and fall right to sleep. Real laborers must sleep soundly.

FEDOTIK

(To Irina) I bought you some colored pencils and a little knife on Moscow Street.

IRINA

You're used to treating me like a little girl, but I'm all grown up! *(Takes the pencils and knife happily)* Oh, they're adorable!

FEDOTIK

And I bought a little knife for myself. See—one, two, three blades. One for digging in your ears, one a little scissors, and this for nail cleaning.

RODÉ

(Loudly) Doctor, how old are you?

CHEBUTYKIN

Me? Thirty-two.

Laughter.

FEDOTIK

Now I'll show you another kind of patience. The card game.

A samovar is brought in by Anfisa. Natasha arrives and bustles around the table. Solyony arrives and sits at the table.

VERSHININ

God, the wind!

MASHA

Yes. I'm sick and tired of winter. I've already forgotten what summer is like.

IRINA

Look, I've won at patience! See the cards? That means we'll go to Moscow.

FEDOTIK

No, you haven't. See, the eight is on the two of spades. *(Laughs)* That means you won't go to Moscow!

CHEBUTYKIN

(Reading the newspaper) An outbreak of smallpox in Tsitsikar.

ANFISA

(Approaching Masha)
Masha, Matushka, tea's ready. *(To Vershinin)* Tea is served, Your Excellency. Forgive me, dear, I've forgotten your name.

MASHA

Bring it here, Nanny. I don't want to go in there.

IRINA

Nanny!

ANFISA

Coming!

NATASHA

Babies who are still breastfeeding understand absolutely *everything.* "Hello, Bobik," I said. "Hello sweetheart!" And he gives me this look—this incredible look . . . of course, you think, she goes on like this because she's his mother. But no, no, I promise you! He really is a remarkable child.

SOLYONY

If that child were mine, I would fry him up in a frying pan and eat him.

Takes his glass and sits in a corner.

NATASHA

(Covering her face) What a rude, badly brought-up man!

MASHA

Happy people don't notice if it's summer or winter. If I were in Moscow, I wouldn't care about the weather.

VERSHININ

The other day I was reading this diary of some French politician, he was convicted of fraud, and wrote it in prison. He talks with such rapture, such delight, about the birds he saw through his prison window. When he was a politician, he never noticed the birds! But, of course, after he's out of jail, he *stops* noticing the birds! If you lived in Moscow, you would cease to *see* Moscow once you actually lived there. See: we can never *have* happiness itself. We can only wish for it, long for it.

TUZENBACH

(Taking a box from the table) Where's the candy?

IRINA

Solyony ate it.

TUZENBACH

All of it?

ANFISA

(Serving tea) A letter came for you, sir.

VERSHININ

For me? *(Takes the letter)* From my daughter. *(Reads)* Yes, of course. Excuse me, Masha. *(To Masha)* I'll just slip out. I won't have tea. *(Getting up)* It's always the same old story.

MASHA

What happened? A secret?

VERSHININ

(In a low voice) My wife poisoned herself again. I must go. I'll slip out, no one will notice. Horribly unpleasant, all of this. *(Vershinin kisses Masha's hand)* My good, sweet kind woman . . . I'll go quietly.

Exits.

ANFISA

Where's he going? I just served the tea! Lord have mercy.

MASHA

(Angrily) Oh, stop it. You're always nosing into our affairs! *(Takes her teacup to the table)* I've had it up to here with you, old woman!

ANFISA

Why are you so offended, dear?

ANDREI

(Offstage) Anfisa!

ANFISA

"Anfisa!" He just sits there.

She exits.

MASHA

(At the table in the dining room, angry) Well, I'll just sit *here*! *(Scatters cards)* Enough with the cards!
Drink your tea.

IRINA

You're being mean, Masha.

MASHA

Well, if I'm mean, don't talk to me. Don't touch me!

CHEBUTYKIN

(Laughing) Don't touch her, don't touch her!

MASHA

You're sixty years old, but you act like a goddamned child.

NATASHA

(Sighing) Masha, dear, why do you use language like that? You have a lovely face, and nice features, and I'm sure you could be charming in society, to be frank, if it weren't for your swearing. *(Pronouncing badly) Je vous prie, pardonnez moi, Marie, mais vous avez des manières un peu grossières.*

TUZENBACH

(Holding back laughter) Pass me . . . pass me—I hope there's cognac there.

The sound of a baby crying.

NATASHA

Il paraît que mon Bobik déjà ne dort pas, he woke up! Oh, dear, he's a little fussy today, I hope he's all right. I'll go check on him. Excuse me.

She exits.

IRINA

But where has the colonel gone?

MASHA

Home. Something's wrong with his wife.

TUZENBACH

(To Solyony, holding cognac)
You're always sitting alone, thinking—thinking God knows what. Look, let's have a truce. Let's have some cognac.

They drink.

TUZENBACH

I'll play the piano all night. I might play a load of garbage. But what the hell!

SOLYONY

What truce? We weren't fighting.

TUZENBACH

You always give me the feeling there's something off between us. You're a strange man, you have to admit.

SOLYONY

(Declaiming) I am strange, but who is not? "Be not angry, Aleko!"

TUZENBACH

Who's Aleko?

Pause.

SOLYONY

When I'm alone with one other person, I feel fine. I'm like anyone else. But in a group, I feel boring and shy, so I enjoy saying utter horseshit. But I'm more honest and noble than most people. And I can prove it.

TUZENBACH

You're always getting on my nerves. And you pick on me in public, constantly, but still, I like you. What the hell. No matter what else happens today, I'm going to get drunk. Let's drink.

SOLYONY

Let's drink.

They drink.

SOLYONY

I never had anything against you, Baron. But I have the soul of a poet who gets killed in a duel. *(Quietly)* In fact, I look like Lermontov . . . or so I've been told . . . *(Takes a bottle of cologne and sprinkles it on his hands)*

TUZENBACH

I handed in my resignation. Enough! For five years, I've been dreaming about it, and finally, it's decided: I'm going to *work*.

SOLYONY

"Be not angry, Aleko! Forget, forget thy dreams . . ."

While they talk, Andrei comes in with his book and sits near a lamp.

TUZENBACH

I will work.

CHEBUTYKIN

(Enters with Irina)
And the food was authentic cuisine from the Caucasus. Onion soup, and for the meat course—chekhmarta.

SOLYONY

Cheremsha isn't meat. It's in the onion family.

CHEBUTYKIN

No, no, no, my angel. Chekhmarta is not an onion, but is, in fact, mutton.

SOLYONY

No, I'm telling you, cheremsha—onion!

CHEBUTYKIN

No, I'm telling *you*: chekhmarta—mutton!

SOLYONY

No, no I'm telling *you*, cheremsha—onion!

CHEBUTYKIN

Why am I arguing with you? You've never been to the Caucasus, and never even eaten chekhmarta!

SOLYONY

I never tried it because I can't stand it. Cheremsha stinks like garlic.

ANDREI

That's enough, you two. Please.

TUZENBACH

When are the carolers coming?

IRINA

They promised to come around nine, so any time now.

Tuzenbach hugs Andrei.
Andrei dances and sings.
Chebutykin joins, dancing.

TUZENBACH, ANDREI AND CHEBUTYKIN
(Perhaps singing in the original Russian):
   Oh, porch, my porch, new porch of mine . . .
   A new porch made of pine
   With criss-crossed wood so fine, so fine—

Laughter.

TUZENBACH

(Kissing Andrei) To hell with it! Let's drink, Andrusha. To friendship! I'll go with you. To Moscow, to the university!

SOLYONY

Which one? There are two universities in Moscow.

ANDREI

There's only one university in Moscow.

SOLYONY

I'm telling you there are two.

ANDREI

Make it three! The more the merrier.

SOLYONY

In Moscow there are *two* universities!

Group expressions of disapproval.

SOLYONY

In Moscow there are two universities, the old and the new. But if you don't want to listen because I annoy you, I'll stop talking. I'll even go to another room. *(Exits)*

TUZENBACH

Bravo, bravo! *(Laughs)*
All right, ladies and gentlemen, let's get started. I'm ready to play. He's a nut, Solyony.

Sits at the piano and plays a waltz. Masha waltzes alone.

MASHA

The Baron is drunk, the Baron is drunk, the Baron is drunk!

Natasha enters.

NATASHA

(To Chebutykin) Ivan Romanych!

She tells him something and exits quietly. Chebutykin taps Tuzenbach on the shoulder and whispers to him.

IRINA

What is it?

CHEBUTYKIN

Time for us to go. Good night, everyone.

TUZENBACH

Good night. Time to go.

IRINA

Wait—what about the carolers?

ANDREI

(Embarrassed) There won't be any carolers. See, my dear, Natasha says Bobik isn't feeling well, and . . . the thing is, I don't know . . . and I decidedly do not care.

IRINA

(Shrugging) Bobik isn't well.

MASHA

Oh well, life goes on, we won't disappear. If they're kicking us out, we'll go. It isn't Bobik who's sick, it's Natasha . . . right here! *(Taps her forehead with her finger)* She's a piece of work.

Andrei exits.

FEDOTIK

Too bad! I was looking forward to a party, but if the child is sick, of course. I'll bring him a little toy tomorrow . . .

RODÉ

(Loud) I purposely took a long nap after lunch today because I thought I'd be dancing all night. And look, it's only nine!

MASHA

Let's go outside. We can talk, figure out something to do.

Voices are heard saying: good night, be well.
The happy laughter of Tuzenbach.
Everyone exits. Anfisa and the maid clear the table and blow the candles.

The nurse is heard singing.
Andrei and Chebutykin enter quietly.
Andrei is dressed in an overcoat and hat.

CHEBUTYKIN

I never managed to get married because life passed me by in a flash, and because I was crazy about your mother, who was already married.

ANDREI

People shouldn't get married. It's boring.

CHEBUTYKIN

True, but it's not lonely. Philosophize all you want, but solitude is a terrible thing, my friend. On the other hand, who gives a shit.

ANDREI

Let's hurry up.

CHEBUTYKIN

Why the rush? We'll get there in time.

ANDREI

I'm afraid my wife will stop us.

CHEBUTYKIN

Ah!

ANDREI

I won't gamble tonight, I'll just sit and watch. I don't feel well. I have this shortness of breath. What should I do for shortness of breath?

CHEBUTYKIN

Don't ask me! I can't remember, my friend. Don't know.

ANDREI

Let's go through the kitchen.

They exit. The doorbell. Voices and laughter.

IRINA

Who is it?

ANFISA

It's the carolers!

The bell rings.

IRINA

Nanny, tell them no one's home, I hope they forgive us.

Anfisa leaves.
Irina walks around the room, lost in thought. Anxious. Solyony enters.

SOLYONY

No one's here. Where is everyone?

IRINA

Gone home.

SOLYONY

That's strange. You're all alone?

IRINA

Yes.

Pause.

Good night.

SOLYONY

I behaved badly earlier, I was being stupid. But you're not like the others—you're pure, above it all, you can see the truth . . . You're the only one who can understand me, you alone. I love, deeply and endlessly love—

IRINA

Good night. Go away.

SOLYONY

I can't live without you. *(Going after her)* My bliss! *(Through tears)* My soul's happiness! Those eyes of yours, those mysterious, stunning, almost-too-bright eyes! I've never seen another woman with eyes anything like yours . . .

IRINA

(Coldly)
Stop it, Vassily Vassilich.

SOLYONY

It's the first time I've spoken to you of love, and I'm not standing on this earth, I'm on another planet. *(Rubs his forehead)* Well, fine. You can't force love. But I won't stand for any rivals. I swear to you by all that's holy, I'll kill the competition. Oh, you beautiful girl!

Natasha approaches with a candle.

NATASHA

(Peers in through one door and crosses past her husband's door) There's Andrei. Oh, let him read. Oh, excuse me, Vasily Vasilych, I didn't know you were here, I'm in my nightgown!

SOLYONY

Who cares. Good-bye!

He exits.

NATASHA

You're tired, sweetheart. Poor thing! *(Kisses Irina)* You should get to bed earlier.

IRINA

Is Bobik sleeping?

NATASHA

He is, but not very well. By the way, dear, I wanted to talk to you. But you're never here, and I never have the time. I think it's too cold and damp in Bobik's nursery. But *your* room is just perfect for a baby. Darling, would you be a love and move in with Olga?

IRINA

(Not understanding) Where?

A sleigh with bells is heard driving up.

NATASHA

You and Olga can share a room, and for now, Bobik can have yours. He's such an angel. Today I said to him, "Bobik-wobik, you're mine, all mine!" And he looked at me with those sweet little eyes.

The doorbell rings.

NATASHA

That's probably Olga. She's so late!

The maid whispers to Natasha.

NATASHA

Protopopov? He's such a riot! Protopopov is outside, and wants me to take a ride with him. In his sleigh. *(Laughs)* Men are funny!

The doorbell rings.

NATASHA

Someone's here. I'll just go for fifteen minutes, a little spin. *(To the maid)* Tell him I'm coming.

The doorbell rings.

NATASHA

Who's ringing? It's probably Olga.

She exits. Irina sits, lost in thought. Kulygin and Olga enter with Vershinin following.

KULYGIN

How do you like that! They said there would be a party!

VERSHININ

That's strange. I just left a little while ago, maybe half an hour, and they were waiting for the carolers.

IRINA

Everyone's gone.

KULYGIN

Masha too? Where could she have gone to? And why is Protopopov downstairs waiting in a sleigh? Who's he waiting for?

IRINA

Don't interrogate me. I'm tired.

KULYGIN

Well, Little-Miss-Princess.

OLGA

My meeting just finished. I'm worn out. Our headmistress is sick,
so I'll have to take her place. Oh, head, my head hurts, my head . . .
(Sits) Yesterday Andrei lost two hundred roubles at cards. The
whole town is talking.

KULYGIN

(Sitting) Yes, even I got tired at that meeting.

VERSHININ

My wife wanted to scare me and she came this close to poisoning
herself. It's all right now, what a relief, I'm happy. Should we
be going? Yes, well, let me wish everyone good night. *(To Kulygin)* Fyodor Illych, come with me somewhere. I can't go home,
I can't. Let's go for a walk.

KULYGIN

I'm tired. I don't want to go anywhere. *(Gets up)* I'm tired. Did
my wife go home?

IRINA

She must have.

KULYGIN

(Kisses Irina's hand) Good night. We can rest tomorrow and the
day after that. Good night! *(Begins to exit)* I want tea. I was plan-

ning to spend the evening in pleasant company and—o fallacem hominum spem! Accusative case exclamatory . . .

VERSHININ

Which means: I will go alone.

Exits with Kulygin, whistling.

OLGA

Head hurts, head . . . Andrei lost. Whole town talking. I'm going to bed. *(Begins to exit)* Tomorrow's a holiday. Oh, God, how lovely that will be! Tomorrow I'm free, the day after I'm free. My head hurts, oh, head.

She exits.

IRINA

Everyone's gone. No one's left.

An accordion is heard.
The nurse sings.

NATASHA

(Entering in a fur coat and hat, crossing through the dining room with the maid following) Home in half an hour! I'll just take the *littlest* ride.

She leaves.

IRINA

(Alone. The verb form of toska*) To Moscow, to Moscow, to Moscow!

Curtain.

---

* "No single word in English renders all the shades of toska. At its deepest and most painful, it is a sensation of great spiritual anguish, often without any specific cause. At less morbid levels it is a dull ache of the soul, a longing with nothing to long for, a sick pining, a vague restlessness, mental throes, yearning. In particular cases it may be the desire for somebody of something specific, nostalgia, love-sickness. At the lowest level it grades into ennui, boredom."—Vladimir Nabokov

Act III

Olga and Irina's bedroom. Their beds are divided with screens.
Two A.M.
Sirens ringing.
No one has gone to bed.
Masha lies on a couch, dressed in black, as usual.

Olga and Anfisa enter.

ANFISA

They're hiding under the stairs, children . . . "Come up now,
come up," I say, "you can't sit there like that." And they cry, saying, "Daddy, we don't know where he is. Please God, don't make
him be all burnt up." Can you imagine! And in the yard, so many
people, half-naked . . .

OLGA

(Taking a dress out of the closet) Here, this grayish one, take it.
And this little one here and this apron too—
This old skirt, take it, Nana.
What in the world is happening! My God!

The whole street must have burned to the ground.
Oh, take this. And this. *(Throwing dresses into Anfisa's arms)*
The poor Vershinins are scared to death,
their house is almost charred to pieces.
They should spend the night with us.
We can't let them go back home. And poor Fedotik—
he lost everything in the fire. He's got nothing.

ANFISA

Why don't you call Ferapont, Olyushka. I can't carry all this.

OLGA

(Ringing for Ferapont) He won't hear.
Someone, come up!

Through the open door a window, red from the fire.
Sirens.

OLGA

What a terrible thing! It's too much.

Ferapont enters.

OLGA

Take these downstairs. Under the stairs, the Kolatinin girls, camped
out. Give them this. And this.

FERAPONT

Yes, ma'am. Moscow burned in 1812. By God! I bet it took those
Frenchies by surprise, willing to burn our own city down instead
of letting the Frogs in.

OLGA

Go on, get moving.

FERAPONT

Yes, ma'am.

Exits.

OLGA

Nana, give everything away. We don't need it. Give it all away.
Nana, I'm tired, hardly standing on my legs . . . We can't let the
Vershinins go home. The little girls can sleep in the living room,
Vershinin downstairs with the Baron; Fedotik too—or let him
stay with us in the hall . . . The doctor is drunk, of course—can
barely stand—we can't let anyone near him. Vershinin's wife—
the living room.

ANFISA

Olyushka, dear, don't put me out of the house! Please!

OLGA

Oh, Nanny, what a silly thing to say, no one is putting you out of
this house.

ANFISA

(Puts her head on Olga's chest) My darling, my little one, you're
like my own . . . I labor, I work! But I'm getting weak, and I hear
everyone say, "Get rid of her!" But where would I go? Where?
I'm over eighty, almost eighty-two . . .

OLGA

Sit, sit. Nanutka. You're tired, poor thing. *(She sits her down)* You
just rest, my good one. You're so pale!

Natasha enters.

NATASHA

I hear they want to create a charity to help the fire victims, as
soon as possible. Why not? It's *such* a good idea. As a general
rule, rich people should help poor people, don't you find? It's the
responsibility of the rich. Bobik and little Sofia dropped off to
sleep with no fuss, as if nothing in the world could ever be wrong.
So many people everywhere! The house is crammed full, I can't
move without bumping into someone. And there's a terrible flu
going around, I'm worried the children will catch it.

OLGA

(Not listening to her) You can't see the fire from here, it's peaceful, this room . . .

NATASHA

Yes. I must look terrible. *(Looking in the mirror)* People say I'm "filling out" in the middle. It's not true! Not a bit! And Masha's asleep, wiped out, poor dear. *(To Anfisa, cold)* How dare you sit when I'm standing right here? Get up! And get out!

Anfisa leaves. A pause.

NATASHA

Why you keep that old lady, I can't for the life of me understand—

OLGA

(Dumbstruck) Excuse me, I do not understand *you*—

NATASHA

She has no purpose at all here. She's a peasant, she should be put out to pasture . . . why do you coddle her! I like order in the house. Useless people have no place in the home. *(Strokes Olga's cheek)* Oh, poor thing, you're all tired out. Our headmistress is tired. When my little Sofia grows up and goes to school, I'll be afraid of you.

OLGA

I won't be headmistress.

NATASHA

Oh, yes you will, Olya. They've decided already.

OLGA

I'll say no . . . I can't . . . I don't have the strength. *(Drinking water)* You were so rude to Nanny . . . I'm sorry, I can't stand it. I can't even see—black dots in front of my eyes . . .

NATASHA

(Anxious) Forgive me, Olya, forgive me . . . I didn't mean to make you mad.

Masha gets up, takes a pillow and leaves, angry.

OLGA

Try to understand, my dear—you might say we were raised strangely, but I will not stand for this. The way you treated her, it makes me sick, chops my soul to bits.

NATASHA

Forgive me, forgive me . . . *(Kisses her)*

OLGA

Even the smallest blunder, a word said without gentleness, it makes my stomach churn.

NATASHA

I say too much. On occasion. But you have to agree with me, my dear: she could go live in the country.

OLGA

She's been with us thirty years.

NATASHA

But she can't work! Either I don't understand you, or you don't want to understand me. She can't *work*. She sleeps, or she sits.

OLGA

So let her sit.

NATASHA

Let her sit? She's a *servant*. *(Through tears)* I don't understand you, Olya. I have a nurse and a wet-nurse; we have a maid, a cook—why do we need that old lady? Why?

A fire alarm rings.

OLGA

This one night and I am ten years older.

NATASHA

Let's come to an understanding, Olya. You live at school, I live at home. You have your teaching, I have a house to run. And when I say something about the servants, well then I know what I'm saying, *I know what I am saying!* . . . And by tomorrow morning, I don't want to see that old bag, that old thief . . . *(Stamping her feet)* . . . that witch! Don't you dare make me mad! Don't you dare! *(Catching herself)* Truly, if you don't move yourself downstairs, we'll be at each other, always. It's terrible.

Kulygin enters.

KULYGIN

Where is Masha? It's high time we went home. The fire, they say, is burning out. *(Stretching)* Only one block burned down—at first, with that wind blowing, it looked as though the whole town would go. *(Sits)* I'm exhausted, Olechka, my dear . . . I often think if it weren't for Masha, I would have married you. You're so good. I'm so tortured. *(Listens for something)*

OLGA

What is it?

KULYGIN

The doctor's on a bender, drinking to get drunk, to spite us. Sounds like he's on his way up—you hear him? Oh, yes, here he comes. Oy, what a one! I'll hide. *(Hides behind a wardrobe in a corner)* The scoundrel!

OLGA

He hasn't had a drop of liquor in two years, suddenly he's completely gone.

Olga and Natasha retreat into a corner of the room.
Chebutykin enters, walking as sober as possible, looks around, walks to the sink and washes his hands.

CHEBUTYKIN

(Morosely) Devil, devils . . . They think I'm a doctor, can cure any disease, but I know positively nothing. I've forgotten everything I knew, every goddamn thing.

To hell with it! Last Wednesday I treated a woman—she died— and it's my fault she died. Yes . . . I used to know something— twenty-five years ago, but now I know nothing. Nothing. My head, it's empty, my soul, it's cold. Maybe I'm not even a man but a walking thing who appears to have arms, legs . . . a head; maybe I don't exist at all, I only think I walk and sleep and eat. *(Cries)* Oh, not to exist! *(Stops crying)* The hell with it. At the club, talking, for a couple of days, they talk Shakespeare, Voltaire. I hadn't read it, none of it, I made this face to look like I had. Others did the same. The pettiness! The pretense! The stupidity! And that woman dead on Wednedsay, she came back to me, everything came back to me . . . and my soul became crooked, ugly, vile . . . I went, I got drunk.

Irina, Vershinin and Tuzenbach enter. Tuzenbach wears civilian clothes, new and stylish.

IRINA

Here, let's sit. No one will come in here.

VERSHININ

If it weren't for the soldiers, the whole town would have burned down! Our brave boys! *(Rubbing his hands)* Slavs—they are a golden people! Our boys!

KULYGIN

(Approaching) What time is it, ladies and gentlemen?

TUZENBACH

After three. It's getting light.

IRINA

Everyone's sitting in the hall, no one's leaving. That Solyony of yours is sitting— *(To Chebutykin)* Doctor, you should go to bed.

CHEBUTYKIN

It's nothing. Thank you, my queen, your highness, thank you. *(Combs his beard)*

KULYGIN

(Laughing) Ivan Romanych, you're officially soused. *(Slaps him on the shoulder)* I commend you! *In vino veritas,* as the ancients would say.

TUZENBACH

I've been asked to put together a concert, to benefit the victims of the fire.

IRINA

But, who is there to . . . ?

TUZENBACH

We could do it, if we want to do it. Masha, in my opinion, plays the piano like a dream.

KULYGIN

That she does!

IRINA

But she's forgotten how. She hasn't played in three years . . . or four . . .

TUZENBACH

No one in this town understands music—not a soul; but me—I do understand it, and I promise you, I do; Masha plays beautifully, masterfully, almost.

KULYGIN

You're right, Baron. I love her very much, my Masha. She is a laudable woman.

TUZENBACH

Imagine, being able to play like that, knowing that no one, not a soul, understands.

KULYGIN

(Sighing) Yes . . . But is it really appropriate for her to play in public?

Pause.

Really, gentlemen, I don't know anything. Maybe it would be good? I confess, although our headmaster is a good man, even a very good man, the most intelligent of men, but he has certain views . . . of course, it's not his business. But, all the same if you'd like, I could perhaps speak with him . . .

Chebutykin picks up a porcelain clock and looks at it.

VERSHININ

In the fire I got covered with dirt. I don't look human.

Pause.

Yesterday I heard a rumor that our brigade is being transferred— some say Poland— others say Siberia.

TUZENBACH

I heard that too. What then? The town will be completely empty.

IRINA

And we'll be gone too!

Chebutykin drops the clock, breaking it.

CHEBUTYKIN

To pieces!

A pause, everyone embarrassed and distressed.

KULYGIN

(Picking up the pieces) Breaking such a valuable thing! Ah, Ivan Romanych, Ivan Romanych! You get a minus *zero* for behavior!

IRINA

That clock was Mama's.

CHEBUTYKIN

Maybe . . . so it was Mama's . . . Maybe I wasn't breaking it, only seems like I broke it. Maybe it only seems like we exist, but really—there is no we . . .

I don't know anything, no one knows anything. What are you all looking at? Natasha is schtupping Protopopov, and you don't see it. You all just sit there not seeing, but Natasha is schtupping Protopopov. *(Singing)* Eat a fig and tell me how you like it! *(Exits)*

VERSHININ

Yes. *(Laughs)* Well, how strange everything is, essentially.

Pause.

When the fire began, I ran home fast as I could, got there, looked . . . our house was out of danger, but my two little girls were standing at the door in their underwear, no mother in sight, people running, horses running, dogs—and I look at the faces of my little girls—panic, terror, a terrible kind of asking, written on their faces—and my heart froze when I saw those faces. My God, I thought, what more will these girls have to live through, in a long life? I grabbed them, ran, thinking one thought: what more will they have to live through in this world?

The fire alarm sounds.

VERSHININ

I come here, their mother's here, screaming, angry.

Masha enters with a pillow and sits down on the sofa.

VERSHININ

And when I saw my little girls standing on the doorstep in their underwear, the street red with fire, the noise terrible, it reminded me of some kind of enemy invasion from long ago, when the army would sack a town, looting and burning as they went. But what a difference between what is and what was! And a little more time will pass, two hundred or three hundred years, and people will look at our current life with horror, with disbelief, and our lives will seem cramped, inconvenient, strange. Oh, what life will be! What a life! *(Laughs)* Forgive me, I'm philosophizing again. But allow me to keep going. I'm dying to philosophize, I'm in the mood.

Pause.

Everyone's asleep.
I say: what a life it will be! You can only imagine . . . Here in this town there are only three people like you now, but in times to come there will be many more, more and more, a time will come when the whole world will tilt in your direction, everyone will live like you, and later, you'll get old, babies will be born who will be better than you! *(Laughs)* I'm in a funny mood today. I want like hell to live . . . *(Singing)* "Everyone must bow to love, cursed or blessed from heaven above, everyone must bow to love—"

MASHA

Trum-tum-tum—

VERSHININ

Tum tum—

MASHA

Tra ra ra?

VERSHININ

Tra ta ta.

He laughs.

Fedotik enters.
He's dancing.

87

FEDOTIK

Burned down, burned clean away! Everything.

Laughter.

IRINA

What is there to joke about? Everything gone?

FEDOTIK

(Laughing through tears) Everything is now nothing! Gone clean away! Nothing left! My guitar burned, my photography burned, all my letters. I wanted to give you a little notebook—it also burned.

Solyony enters.

IRINA

No. Please leave, Vassily Vassilyitch. You can't come in.

SOLYONY

Why can the Baron enter, and not me?

VERSHININ

We should all go, really. How's the fire?

SOLYONY

They say it's dying down. No, really, it's very strange to me: why can the Baron enter, and not me?

Solyony sprinkles himself with perfume.

VERSHININ

Tram-tum-tum.

MASHA

Tram-tum.

VERSHININ

(Laughing to Solyony) Come on, let's go to the hall.

SOLYONY

Very well, my dear sir. I've taken note. I would further explain this thought, but I fear the chicken would cheep. *(Solyony stares at Tuzenbach)* Cheep cheep cheep.

He exits with Vershinin and Fedotik.

IRINA

Solyony smoked the whole room up! *(Startled)* The Baron's asleep! Baron! Baron!

TUZENBACH

(Waking) Sleep, sleepy, oh but the brick factory . . . I'm not talking in my sleep, I'm not . . . In real life, I am going to the brick factory, to start work . . . I spoke with them already . . . You're so pale, so beautiful, so charming . . . your skin lightens the dark air, like a lamp . . . You're sad, you're not satisfied with life. Oh, come away with me, come away, and we'll work together!

MASHA

Nikolay Lvovitch, leave.

TUZENBACH

(Laughing) You're here? I didn't see you. *(Kissing Irina's hand)* Good-bye, I'm going . . . I look at you now and I remember the day of your birthday, some time ago, when you were so full of joy, and life, rhapsodizing about labor . . . What a happy life appeared before my eyes then! Where is it? *(Kisses her hand)* You have tears in your eyes. Go to bed . . . it's getting light . . . morning is beginning . . . if only I were allowed to give my life for you!

MASHA

Nikolay Lvovitch, leave! Truly.

TUZENBACH

I'm going . . .

He leaves.

MASHA

(Lying down) Are you asleep, Fydor?

KULYGIN

Huh?

MASHA

You should go home.

KULYGIN

Masha, my Masha-mine . . .

IRINA

She's exhausted . . . Let her rest, Fedya.

KULYGIN

I'll go now . . . My wife is a good woman, a laudable woman . . . I love you, my only one . . .

MASHA

(Angry) Amo, amas, amat, amamus, amatis, amant.

KULYGIN

No, it's true, she's really remarkable. I've been married to you for seven years, but it feels like yesterday we took our vows. On my word, it's true, you're a remarkable woman. I'm content, content, content!

MASHA

I'm fed up, up up! *(Sitting up)* I can't get it out of my head. It's shocking. Like a nail sticking in my skull, I can't be silent. I mean Andrei . . . He mortgaged this house to the bank, his wife takes all the money, but this house isn't *his*, it belongs to the four of us! He would know that, if he were a decent human being.

KULYGIN

Nothing to do, Masha, nothing to do. Andryusha's caught in a circle of bad loans . . . his debt is crushing him . . . God help him.

MASHA

In any case, it's shocking. *(She lies back down)*

KULYGIN

You and I aren't poor. I work, I teach, I tutor. I'm an honest man. A simple man. *Omnia mea mecum porto*, as they say.

MASHA

I don't need a single thing, it's the injustice that makes me want to scream.

Pause.

Go home, Fyodor.

KULYGIN

(Tries to kiss her) You're tired. Rest a little, I'll sit out there and wait. Sleep . . .
(He goes)
I'm content, I'm content, I'm content.

IRINA

Really, Andrei gets smaller the more he grows up, how dried up he is around that woman! He was going to be a *professor*, and yesterday he was bragging that he had finally become a full member of the county council. He's a member of the county council, Protopopov is his boss . . . the whole town is talking, the whole town is laughing, and he alone sees nothing, knows nothing. And now, everyone's run to help fight the fire, and he sits alone in his room, paying no attention. He only plays the violin.
Oh, it's horrible, horrible, horrible! *(Crying)* I can't, I can't *carry* this anymore! . . . I can't, I can't . . .

Olga enters, tidying.

IRINA

(Sobbing) Throw me out, throw me, I can't anymore . . .

OLGA

What is it, what is it, love?

IRINA

(Sobbing) Where? Where has it all gone? Where is it?
Oh, God, my God!
I've forgotten everything, I forgot . . .
my head is foggy—
I don't remember the Italian word for *window*—
or for ceiling—
I'm forgetting everything, every day forgetting, and
life leaves us and doesn't come back, never—
never going to Moscow—
I see now that we will not go . . .

OLGA

Milaya, milaya . . .
(Or: Sweet one, sweet . . .)

IRINA

Oh, I'm so unhappy. *(Restraining herself)*
I can't work, I won't work.
Enough, enough.
First I was a telegraph clerk, now I work for the city council
and I hate every little thing they make me do.
I'm getting older, it feels like I've been working forever,
my brain's drying up.
I've become thin, stupid and old.
There's nothing nothing—no reward for it—
no fullness—satisfaction—
and as time passes, you move further and further away
from a real and beautiful life, moving and moving
toward some black pit.
I feel desperate, and how it is that I'm alive, how it is I haven't
killed myself by now,
I don't understand.

OLGA

Don't cry, my girl, don't cry. I can't bear it.

IRINA

I'm not crying, not crying . . . Enough . . . See, I'm already not crying. That's enough.

OLGA

Sweetheart, as your sister, and as a friend, if you want my advice, marry the Baron!

Irina cries quietly.

You respect him. You value him. True, he's not the best looking, but he's so *decent,* so clean . . . People don't marry for love, they marry for duty. At least, that's what I think, and I'd get married without being in love. As long as he was decent, who cares, I'd even marry an old man.

IRINA

I've been waiting for us to move to Moscow, where I'd meet my soul mate, my beloved, I've already dreamed of him, I loved . . . But it turns out that was stupid, so stupid.

OLGA

(Embracing her sister) I understand. I do. When the Baron left the army and visited us in that civilian jacket, he looked so plain even I started to cry. He asked, "Why are you crying?" What could I tell him! But if God joined the two of you in marriage, I'd be happy. That would be an entirely different thing!

Natasha appears and walks from right to left, holding a candle.

MASHA

She walks around with that candle like she was the one who started the fire.

OLGA

Masha, you're stupid. The stupidest one in our family: excuse me, but it's you.

Pause.

MASHA

I want to make a confession, dear sisters. My soul is so tired. I'll confess to you and to no one else, never . . . I'll tell you this minute. *(Quietly)* It's my secret, but you must know. I can't be silent.

I love, love . . . love that man . . . You just saw him . . . That's that. In a word: I love—Vershinin.

OLGA

(Goes off behind her screen)
Stop it. Or go on, either way, I'm not listening.

MASHA

What can be done? *(Takes her head in her hands)* First, he seemed strange to me, then I felt pity for him . . . then I fell in love with him. I fell in love with his voice, his words—his unhappiness . . . And his two girls . . .

OLGA

I can't hear you! Keep saying stupid things, it doesn't matter, I'm not listening.

MASHA

Ay, you're stupid, Olya. I love—it's my fate. Or my one job in this life . . . And he loves me . . . It's terrifying. Yes? But is it wrong?
(Pulling Irina's hand to her) Oh, my dear . . . Somehow we will live through our lives . . .
When you read a novel, it seems that everything is clear, trite and understandable. But when you yourself fall in love, you understand that nobody knows anything and everyone must decide for themselves. Sweet sisters, I made my confession, now I'll shut

up . . . I will now be like the crazy man in Gogol—Silence . . . silence . . .

Andrei enters, followed by Ferapont.

ANDREI

(Angry) What do you want? I don't understand.

FERAPONT

Andrei Sergeyevitch, I've told you ten times.

ANDREI

First of all, I'm not Andrei Sergeyevitch to you but "Your Excellency"!

FERAPONT

The firemen, My Most Excellentness, request permission to go through your garden to get to the river. As it is, they're going round and around in circles, like a punishment.

ANDREI

Fine, tell them it's fine.

Ferapont leaves.

ANDREI

I'm fed up.
Where's Olga?

Olga comes out from behind the screen.

ANDREI

I came to ask you for the key to the cupboard. I lost mine. You have that—tiny little key.

Olga gives him the key without speaking.
Irina goes behind her screen.
A pause.

ANDREI

What a crazy fire! It's starting to die down now. I'll be damned, Ferapont's made me so mad. I said something stupid to him . . . Your Excellency . . . Why are you so quiet, Olya?

It's time you stopped this stupidity and acting like some aloof princess. You and Masha are here, Irina's here . . . excellent, let's come clean, once and for all. What do you have against me? What?

OLGA

Leave it be, Andrusha. Tomorrow we'll have it out. What a terrible night.

ANDREI

Don't get emotional. I'm asking you now—I am completely cold-blooded: what have you got against me? Give it to me straight.

VERSHININ

(From offstage) Tram tam tam!

MASHA

(Gets up, loudly) Tra ta ta!
Good-bye, Olya. God bless you.
(Goes behind screen, kisses Irina)
Sleep well, good night.
Good-bye, Andrei. Leave, they're exhausted . . . tomorrow you can have it out.

She exits.

OLGA

Really, Andrei, let's leave it for tomorrow. *(Goes behind screen)* Time to sleep.

ANDREI

I'll say it, and go. Now . . . first, you have something against Natasha, my wife. I've watched you judging her ever since our wedding day. Natasha is a beautiful, honest woman, direct and—

noble in my opinion. My wife, I love and respect my wife, and I demand that others respect her, as I do. I repeat: she's an honest, honorable woman and all of your nitpicking, excuse me for saying so, is sheer capriciousness.

In the second place, you seem annoyed that I'm not a professor, that I don't fill my life with science. But I'm a member of government, of the county council, and I consider my service as holy and lofty as serving science. I'm a full member of the county council, and I'm proud of it, if you want to know . . .

Thirdly . . . one more thing . . . I mortgaged the house without asking your permission . . . and, in that, I'm guilty, I know, and I ask you to forgive me. I was forced to, by these never-ending loans . . . Thirty-five thousand. I'm already not gambling. I gave it up, long ago, but what's more important, what I can say in my own defense, is that you girls receive pensions, while I don't have any . . . salary, so to speak.

KULYGIN

(At the door) Masha's not here? *(Worried)* Where is she? That's strange . . .

He leaves.

ANDREI

You're not listening. Natasha is a most—excellent—honest—person.
When I got married, I thought we'd be happy . . . everyone happy . . . but, oh my God! . . .
(Crying)
My sweet sisters, don't believe me, don't believe . . .

He exits.

KULYGIN

(At the door, anxiously) Where is Masha? Masha's not here? How very strange, how strange indeed!

He exits.
The fire alarm sounds, the stage is empty.

IRINA

(Behind the screen) Olya! Who's knocking on the floor?

OLGA

The doctor. He's drunk.

IRINA

There is no peace, this night . . .

Pause.

Olya! *(She looks from behind the screen)*
Did you hear? They're taking the army away from us, sending them somewhere far away.

OLGA

It's only a rumor.

IRINA

We'll be left alone—
Olya!

OLGA

Yes?

IRINA

My dear, sweet Olya, I respect—I very much value—the Baron; he's a beautiful person, I'll marry him, I give my word, only let's go to Moscow! I beg you, let's go! There is nothing better on this green earth than Moscow! Let's go, Olya! Let's go!

Act IV

A garden by the house.
Fir trees. A river in sight.
A veranda with bottles and glasses,
someone has been drinking champagne.
Noon.
Passersby occasionally cut through the garden from the street to the river.
Five or so soldiers pass quickly by.
Chebutykin, in fine spirits throughout the act,
sits in an armchair in the garden,
wearing a cap and holding a walking stick.
Irina, Kulygin with a medal around his neck,
and Tuzenbach on the veranda,
saying good-bye to Fedotik and Rodé, both wearing officer's uniforms.

TUZENBACH
(Kissing Fedotik) You're a good man, we all lived so easily together, as friends.
(Kissing Rodé)
One more time, farewell, my friend!

IRINA

Good-bye.

FEDOTIK

Not good-bye, but farewell, we'll never meet again.

KULYGIN

Who knows? *(Wiping his eyes and smiling)* Oh, now, I'm starting to cry . . .

IRINA

We'll meet again some day.

FEDOTIK

In ten or fifteen years? But by then we'll hardly know each other, we'll greet each other like strangers. *(He takes a picture)* Hold still, one more, last time.

RODÉ

(Embracing Tuzenbach) We won't meet again. *(Kisses Irina's hand)* Thank you for everything, everything!

FEDOTIK

Hold still!

TUZENBACH

If God is good, we will meet again. Write us. You must write.

RODÉ

(Looking around the garden) Good-bye trees!
(He shouts to produce an echo)
Oooooooh!
Good-bye, echo!

KULYGIN

I'm afraid you'll get married off in Poland . . . You'll have a Polish wife who will embrace you and whisper, "*Kochany*!" That's: "My darling . . ." in Polish! *(He laughs)*

FEDOTIK

(Looking at his watch) Not even an hour left.

Solyony's the only one from our unit going on the boat, the rest of us are marching.

Today three units leave, tomorrow another three, and then this town will be back to peace and quiet.

TUZENBACH

And extreme boredom.

RODÉ

Where is Masha?

KULYGIN

In the garden.

FEDOTIK

We must say good-bye to her.

RODÉ

Good-bye, I need to go now or I'll cry . . . *(He quickly embraces Tuzenbach and Kulygin, kisses Irina's hand)* We lived beautifully here . . .

FEDOTIK

(To Kulygin) Something to remember us . . . a little notebook and a tiny pencil . . . We'll go this way to the river . . .

RODÉ

(Shouting to produce an echo) Geddy-uuuuuuup!

KULYGIN

(Shouting) Good-bye!

Fedotik and Rodé see Masha far off and say good-bye. They exit.

IRINA

They're gone . . .

She sits on the bottom of the terrace, close to the ground, the lowest step, along the road, like a stoop.

CHEBUTYKIN

And forgot to say good-bye to me.

IRINA

What about you to them?

CHEBUTYKIN

Oh, I somehow forgot. In any case, I'll see them soon, I'll leave tomorrow. Yes . . . only one more little day left. In a year they'll give me a pension, I'll retire, come back here and live out my century near you. Just one more little year, then I get my pension *(He puts one newspaper in his pocket and takes out another)* I'll come back here to you and change my life from the bottom up. Become a quiet, respectable little thing . . .

IRINA

Well, you should change your life somehow, my little dove. You really should.

CHEBUTYKIN

Yes, I feel that too. *(Singing)* Tarara boom de-ay . . . think I'll sit down de-yay!

KULYGIN

You're incorrigible, Ivan Romanitch, incorrigible . . .

CHEBUTYKIN

Be my teacher then. For you, I'll be corrigible.

IRINA

Fyodor has shaved his mustache, I can't look at him.

KULYGIN

Why not?

CHEBUTYKIN

I would say what your physiognomy now resembles . . . but, oh, I can't.

KULYGIN

So what! It's an accepted hairstyle, a shaved face is the *modus vivendi*. Our headmaster's already shaved his mustache, and when I got promoted, I shaved mine too! No one likes it, but for me, I don't care. I'm content. With a mustache, without a mustache, I'm equally content.

Kulygin sits.
In the back of the garden, Andrei pushes a baby carriage.

IRINA

Ivan Romanitch, my little dove, I'm terribly worried. You were on the boulevard yesterday, tell me, what happened?

CHEBUTYKIN

What happened? Oh, nothing. Silliness. *(Reads his newspaper)* So what.

KULYGIN

They say that Solyony and the Baron met yesterday on the boulevard outside the theater . . .

TUZENBACH

Stop it! That's enough— *(Waves his hand and goes into the house)*

KULYGIN

Outside the theater . . . Solyony was taunting the Baron, and the Baron wouldn't stand for it, and said something insulting—

CHEBUTYKIN

I wouldn't know. It's crap.

KULYGIN

This one time, at the university, a professor wrote in the margins of a student paper: "crap!" And the student misread it in Latin, thought it said "carpe" and tried to conjugate it—carpo, car-pere, carpsi, carptum . . . *(He laughs)* Delightfully funny. They say Solyony is in love with Irina, and so hates the Baron. That's understandable. Irina is a very good girl. She's even a bit like Masha, she's a thinking person, she gets lost in thought. But you have a more gentle temperament, Irina. Of course Masha has a fine temperament. I love her, my Masha.

From the garden: "Aoooooooo! Geddy-up!"

IRINA

(Shivering) Everything scares me today, somehow.

My things are all packed, after dinner I'll send them off.
Tomorrow the Baron and I will be married, tomorrow we move to the brick factory and the day after tomorrow I'll start school, a new life is beginning. Somehow God will help me!
When I passed the teacher's exam, I cried with joy . . .
and gratitude . . .
Now they're here to get my things.

KULYGIN

Yes indeed, you have a good deal of idealism, but you lack seriousness. Lots of ideas; very little seriousness. And yet, I wish you well, from my soul.

CHEBUTYKIN

(Moved) My good one, my golden one, you've gone far away. I can't catch up. I'm left behind, like some migrating bird that got too old, that can't fly. Fly away, my girls, fly with God!
It was a big mistake, Fyodor Ilyitch, to shave your mustache.

KULYGIN

Enough! *(Sighing)* Well, today the officers leave, and everything will go on as before. I don't care what anyone says, Masha's a good, honest woman and I love her and I'm grateful for my fate. Everyone . . . fate is different for different people—I know this one man, he works for the taxation bureau. We went to school together, but they expelled him sophomore year because he never could wrap his head around *ut consecutivum*. Now he's got no money, he's very ill, and when we meet, I say, "Greetings, ut consecutivum." "Yes," he says, "indeed, consecutivum," then he coughs . . . But me, I've been lucky, all my life, and happy—I have the Order of Stanislav, Second Class, and now I teach others the *ut consecutivum*. Of course I'm an intelligent person, maybe more intelligent than a good many, but intelligence doesn't make happiness, no . . .

Inside someone plays the piano, the Maiden's Prayer, a simple, sentimental song.

IRINA

And tomorrow night I won't be hearing that dumb song on the piano anymore,
and I won't be bumping into Protopopov . . .
Protopopov is just sitting there in the living room. He stopped by again today.

KULYGIN

And where is our headmistress?

Masha strolls in the background.

IRINA

Not here. We sent for her.
If only you knew how hard it is for me to be here alone without Olya. She lives at that school, playing headmistress, busy with work all day long, and here I'm alone, bored out of my mind, the walls of my room disgust me. I've made up my mind: if I'm not destined to go to Moscow, then let it be.
It's fate, nothing to be done.
Everything is God's will, it is.
Nikolai proposed to me.
So?
I thought it over, I decided.
He's a good person, almost shocking, how good he is . . .

And suddenly it was like my soul acquired wings,
I got happier, and happier, and light—
And felt again the desire for work work . . .
But only yesterday, something happened, a hidden thing hanging
over me . . .

CHEBUTYKIN

Crapo, crapsi, craptum.

NATASHA

(Out the window) Our headmistress!

KULYGIN

The headmistress has arrived. Let's go inside.

Exits with Irina into the house.

CHEBUTYKIN

(Reading the newspaper and mumbling to himself) Tararaboom-
deaye . . . think I'll sit down de-aye . . .

Masha approaches.
Andrei is in the background, pushing the baby carriage.

MASHA

There he sits, and sits and sits . . .

CHEBUTYKIN

So what?

MASHA

Nothing . . .
Did you love my mother?

CHEBUTYKIN

Very much.

MASHA

And she you?

CHEBUTYKIN

(After a pause) That I already don't remember.

MASHA

Is my man here? That's how our cook Marta spoke of her police-man: "my man." Is my man here?

CHEBUTYKIN

Not yet.

MASHA

When you snatch happiness in little bits, fits and starts, and lose it, like me, you become coarse, little by little, you become hateful. *(Pointing to her breast)* Right here, in me, it's boiling . . . *(Looking at Andrei with the baby carriage)* Look at Andrei, our brother . . . all hopes fallen away. In the Red Square, thousands of people lifted an enormous bell together, huge amounts of labor, and money, and suddenly it falls, it breaks. Suddenly, for no reason. Like Andrei.

ANDREI

When, when will there be quiet in this house again? What a racket.

CHEBUTYKIN

Soon.
(Winding his watch)
I have a very old watch, see, it chimes.
(It chimes)
The first, second, and fifth units are leaving at one o'clock sharp. And me—tomorrow.

ANDREI

For good?

CHEBUTYKIN

Don't know. Maybe in a year, who the hell knows, it's all the same.

Somewhere far off a harp and a fiddle are playing.

ANDREI

The whole town is disappearing, exactly as if it were a tray of food, being covered with one of those huge metal lids.

Pause.

Something happened yesterday in front of the theater; everyone's talking, but I don't know.

CHEBUTYKIN

Nothing. Silliness. Solyony was picking on the Baron and the Baron exploded and called him a name and in the end Solyony was obliged to challenge him to a duel. *(Looking at his watch)* It's already time now, it seems. Half past twelve, in the clearing, the one you can see from here, past the river . . . Pop pop! *(Laughing)* Solyony fancies himself a Lermontov, and even writes poetry. A joke is a joke, but this is already his third duel.

MASHA

Whose?

CHEBUTYKIN

Solyony's.

MASHA

And the Baron?

CHEBUTYKIN

What about the Baron?

MASHA

I'm confused. In any case, I say: they shouldn't be allowed to do this. He might wound the Baron, or even kill him.

CHEBUTYKIN

The Baron is a good man but one Baron more, one Baron less— what's the big difference? Let them! No difference!

In the garden shouts of: "Aooooo aoooo, geddyup!"

CHEBUTYKIN

Wait, wait.

That's Skvortsov, playing Solyony's second. He's sitting in a boat.

ANDREI

To me, taking part in a duel, even to be present *at* a duel, as a doctor, is quite simply immoral.

CHEBUTYKIN

Only seems that way. We're not really here, nothing exists in this world, not even us, it only seems that we do. Isn't it all the same . . .

MASHA

All day long: talk, talk, talk . . .

(Going)

You live in this climate, every time you look up it's snowing, and on top of it, we have to *talk* . . .

(Stopping)

I'm not going in the house, I can't . . .

When Vershinin comes, tell me . . .

(Walking up a path)

The migrating birds are off . . . flying . . .

(Looking up)

Swans or geese—

Sweet ones, happy ones!

She goes out.

ANDREI

Our house will be empty.

The officers will go, you will go,

My sister will go and get married, and I'm staying in the house, all alone.

CHEBUTYKIN

What about your wife?

Ferapont enters.

ANDREI

A wife is a wife. She's honest, decent—well, good in her way—
but she has something in her that reduces her to a petty, blind,
crude little animal. In any case, she isn't a person. I say this to you
as a friend, the only person I can open my soul to. I love Natasha,
I do, but sometimes she seems to me incredibly vulgar, and then
I get lost, lose myself, I don't understand what I love her for, or
why—I love her so—or—at least, loved—

CHEBUTYKIN

(Rising) Brother, I'm leaving tomorrow, we may never meet
again, so, a word of advice: put on a hat, carry a big stick, and
go—be off, go, without a glance back. And the further you get
the better.

Solyony walks by the rear with two officers; he turns to Chebutykin.

SOLYONY

Doctor, it's time. Twelve-thirty already.

Solyony waves to Andrei.

CHEBUTYKIN

Coming. I'm sick of you all. *(To Andrei)* If anyone asks for me,
Andrusha, say that I'm— *(He sighs)*

SOLYONY

A man can't breathe in any case
When a brown bear comes and sits on his face.

(Walking with Chebutykin) Why the groaning, old man?

CHEBUTYKIN

So!

SOLYONY

How's the health?

CHEBUTYKIN

(Angry) Like butter from a cow!

SOLYONY

The old man is getting upset for no reason. I'll just indulge myself a wee bit, I'll only nip his wing like a wood-snipe. *(Sprinkling perfume on his hands)* See, today, I poured out a whole bottle, and still they smell. Smell like a corpse.
Remember the poem?

The restless soul seeks out a storm
As if in storms were in-laid peace

CHEBUTYKIN

A man can't breathe in any case
When a brown bear comes and sits on his face.

Shouts are heard, Andrei and Ferapont enter.

FERAPONT

Papers to sign . . .

ANDREI

Leave me alone! Go away please! I beg you.

Andrei exits with the baby carriage.

FERAPONT

What else are papers for, but to be signed.

Ferapont exits.
Enter Irina and Tuʒenbach, Tuʒenbach in a straw hat.
Kulygin crosses the stage, calling: "Aoooo, Masha, Aoooo!"

TUZENBACH

The only man in town who's happy to see the soldiers go.

IRINA

It's understandable.
Our town will be empty now.

TUZENBACH

(Looking at his watch) Sweet girl, I'll come right back.

IRINA

Where are you going?

TUZENBACH

I have to go into town . . . see my comrades off.

IRINA

That's not true . . . Nikolai, why are you so distracted today?
What happened yesterday, by the theater?

TUZENBACH

(With an impatient gesture) In an hour I'll be back and I'll be with
you again.
(Kissing her hand)
Beloved . . .
(Looking into her face)
Five years of loving you and I'm still not used to it,
you seem always more and more beautiful.
What beautiful, wonderful hair!
What eyes!
I'll whisk you away tomorrow,
We'll work, we'll get rich,
my dreams will come alive.
You will be happy.
Only there's one, one thing—
you don't love me.

IRINA

That's not in my power!
I'll be a good wife, I'll be faithful and humble
but there's no love, what can I do?

(She cries)
I've never been in love, never in my life.
Oh, I've dreamed of love, dreamed endlessly, day and night,
but my soul is like a fine piano that's locked,
and the key is lost.

You look restless.

TUZENBACH

I've not slept.
There's nothing in my life so terrible that I'm scared of it,
but that lost key is lodged in my soul—won't let me sleep.
Say something to me . . .

IRINA

What? What can I say? The trees are so quiet, everything hidden
from us, even the secrets of trees . . .

She puts her head on his chest.

TUZENBACH

Say something to me . . .

IRINA

What? What should I say? What?

TUZENBACH

Something.

IRINA

Enough . . . enough!

Pause.

TUZENBACH

What silly little things sometimes take on meaning in life, suddenly, out of nowhere. And you know they're little nothings, and
you laugh at them, but all the same, you go on feeling them, you
can't stop . . .

Oh, let's not talk about it! I feel happy. I see, as if for the first time in my life, these firs, maples, birch trees—and they all look back at me, curious, waiting.

What beautiful trees, and what a beautiful life should be lived under their branches!

A shout is heard: "Aaooooo, geddyup!"

TUZENBACH

Time to go. It's time.
That tree is dead but it's still moving with the others in the wind.
So, if I die, I'll still be part of life, one way or another.
Good-bye, my dear—
(Kisses her hand)
The papers you gave me are on my table, under the calendar.

IRINA

But I'll go with you.

TUZENBACH

(Alarmed) No, no!
(Leaving quickly, then stopping)
Irina!

IRINA

What?

TUZENBACH

(Not knowing what to say) I didn't drink my coffee today. Ask them to make me some.

He exits, quickly.
Irina stands, thinking, then sits down in the swing.
Andrei enters with the baby carriage.
Ferapont enters.

FERAPONT

But Andrei Sergevitch, these aren't my papers, they're official, I didn't dream them up.

114

ANDREI

(Almost threatening the audience with his fists) Oh, where is it, where did my past go, when I was young, happy and intelligent, when my dreams and thoughts had some grace, and the present and future were lit up with hope? Why is it, that when we've just started to live, we grow dull, gray, uninteresting, lazy, useless, with flattened-out souls? Our town has been around for two hundred years, a hundred thousand people live in it, and there's not a single one who's not just like all the others, not one that stands out, past or present, not one scholar, not one artist, not one mildly remarkable person, who would arouse envy, or passionate imitation. They only eat, drink, sleep, and die. Others are born— they too eat, drink and sleep, and, to save themselves from insane boredom, they find variety in vicious gossip, vodka, cards, and pointless lawsuits, and wives deceive their husbands, husbands lie too, pretending not to see or hear, and this vulgarity inevitably wears away at the children, and God's spark dies out in them. They become the same sad homogenous corpses as their fathers, and their mothers . . .

(To Ferapont, angry)
What do you want?

FERAPONT

What? Papers to sign.

ANDREI

I'm sick of you.

FERAPONT

(Handing over the papers) Just now the doorman at the taxation bureau was saying . . . it seems that last winter in St. Petersburg the temperature was two hundred below.

ANDREI

The present is disgusting, but when I imagine the future—oh, how good! It becomes easy, spacious, in the distance, a little piece of light, I see freedom, how my children and I will be free from idleness, from beer, from goose and cabbage, from epic post-prandial naps, from being sick leeches . . .

FERAPONT

They say two thousand people froze. People were scared out of their wits. St. Petersburg or Moscow—can't remember . . .

ANDREI

(Suddenly tender) My dear sisters, my good sisters! *(Through tears)* Masha, my sister . . .

Natasha appears in a window.

NATASHA

Who's talking so loud! Is it you, Andrusha? You'll wake Sophie. *Il ne faut pas faire du bruit, la Sofie est dormie déjà. Vous êtes un ours. (Getting angry)* If you want to talk, give the carriage to someone else. Ferapont, take the carriage.

FERAPONT

Yes, ma'am.

He takes the carriage.

ANDREI

(Embarassed) I am talking quietly.

Natasha from behind the window, teasing her child.

NATASHA

Bobik! Naughty little Bobik! Baddy Bobik!

ANDREI

(Looking through the papers) Fine, fine, I'll look at them and sign what I need to sign, then you can bring them back to the council . . .

He goes into the house, reading the papers.
Ferapont pushes the carriage.
Vershinin, Olga and Anfisa emerge from the house, and listen quietly for a moment.
Irina joins them.

ANFISA

Iri, hello!
(Kisses her. Clicks her tongue)
My child, how I live! How I live!
In a brand-new government apartment, at the high school,
with Olya— God has blessed me in my old age.
From birth, sinner that I am . . . I've never lived like this—
A big apartment, the government pays, a whole room to myself
and a little bed.
It's all on the government! I wake up in the night—and oh Lord,
oh mother of God, no one's happier than me.

VERSHININ

(After looking at his watch) We're leaving now, Olga Sergeyevna.
It's time.
I wish you everything, everything.
Where's Maria Sergeyevna?

IRINA

She's off in the garden. I'll find her.

VERSHININ

If you would, please. I must hurry.

ANFISA

I'll help look. *(Calling)* Mashenka! Yoo hoo!

Going to the rear of the garden with Irina.

VERSHININ

Well, everything ends. And here we are, saying good-bye.
(Looks at his watch)
The town gave us a send-off, a little lunch, champagne, the mayor
speechified. I ate and listened, but my heart was here with you all . . .
I've grown so used to you . . .

OLGA

Will we ever meet again?

VERSHININ

Probably not.

My wife and two girls will be here for another month or so before leaving. Please, if anything happens, or if it's necessary to . . .

OLGA

Yes, yes of course. Not to worry.

By tomorrow there won't be a single officer in town;
all will be a memory.

And of course, for us, a new life begins.

Nothing turns out the way we plan.

I didn't want to be a headmistress and here I am, a headmistress.

Moscow—it's not to be.

VERSHININ

Well . . . Thank you for everything. Forgive me, if anything wasn't quite right, I talked too much, much too much, forgive me for that too. Don't think ill of me.

OLGA

(Wiping her eyes) Oh . . . why isn't Masha coming . . .

VERSHININ

What more can I say to you instead of saying good-bye? I could philosophize for you . . . *(Laughs)* Life's hard. It can look so dim, so grim, but doesn't it get clearer and more light? One day it will be perfectly light. *(Looks at his watch)* Time for me to go, it's time! Used to be men were utterly consumed with war, our whole existence was filled with marches, invasions, conquests—now all of that's over, leaving in its wake a big empty space, waiting to be filled in. Mankind searches passionately for the filling, and of course will find it one day. Ach, let it be soon!

If only we could add the love of wisdom to the love of labor, and the love of labor to the love of wisdom . . .

Looking at his watch.

VERSHININ

But my time is up.

OLGA

Here she comes.

Masha enters.

VERSHININ

I came to say good-bye . . .

Olga withdraws.
Masha looks at Vershinin's face.

MASHA

Good-bye . . .

A long kiss.

OLGA

Let it be, let it be . . .

Masha sobs violently.

VERSHININ

Write to me . . . Don't forget! Let me go . . . it's time . . . Olga, take her, I already . . . have to go—it's time . . . late . . .

Deeply moved, he kisses Olga's hand and embraces Masha again and leaves quickly.

OLGA

Let it be! Stop, sweet Masha.

Kulygin enters.

KULYGIN

(Embarrassed) It's all right, let her cry a little, let her . . . My good Masha, my kind Masha . . . You're my wife, and I'm happy,

whatever happened . . . I'm not complaining . . . I won't give you
a single bad mark. Olga as my witness . . . We'll start over again
living as we used to live, and I won't say a word, not a single
syllable . . .

MASHA

(Reigning in her sobs)
By the bending sea, a green oak tree—
Where a golden chain is bound—
Golden chain is bound . . . I'm losing my mind,
Bending sea, green oak tree—

OLGA

Be peaceful, Masha, calm down . . . give her water.

MASHA

I'm not crying anymore . . .

KULYGIN

She's not crying . . . she's a good one . . .

A shot is heard faintly from far off.

MASHA

By the bending sea, a green oak tree,
Where a golden chain is bound
And on that tree a cultured cat
goes round and round and round—
a green cat, a green oak

I'm mixing it all up . . .

She takes a drink of water.

It's an unlucky life . . . now I don't want a thing. I'll soon be calm.
It's all the same.
What does it mean, a bending sea?

Why is that phrase stuck in my head?
My thoughts are foggy.

Irina enters.

OLGA

Calm yourself, Masha, there's a good girl, let's go inside.

MASHA

(Angry) I won't go in there!
(Sobbing, then stopping)
I don't go in that house anymore and I won't go!

IRINA

Let's sit together, and let's be quiet.
Tomorrow I'm going away . . .

Pause.

KULYGIN

Yesterday I took this mustache and beard away from a sophomore
. . . *(He puts on the mustache and beard)* I look like the German
teacher. *(Laughing)* Don't you think? Those boys, so silly . . .

MASHA

You really do look like the German.

OLGA

(Laughing) Yes!

Masha weeps.

IRINA

What will be will be. There, Masha!

KULYGIN

A lot like—

Natasha enters.

NATASHA

(To the maid) So? Protopopov—that is to say, Mikhail Ivanitch—will sit with Sophie, and Andrei can take Bobik for a walk. It never ends with children!

(To Irina) Irina, you leave tomorrow, what a shame! Stay for one more week, won't you?

(Sees Kulygin and screams.
He laughs and takes his mustache and beard off)
You scared me half to death!

(To Irina) I've gotten used to you, do you think letting you go will be easy on me?

I told the servants to move Andrei and his violin into your room—let him play play play in there!—and in Andrei's room we'll put my sweet Sophie. She's such a divine, miraculous child. What a dumpling pie! Today she looked at me with these *eyes* and said: Mama!

KULYGIN

A beautiful child, without a doubt.

NATASHA

So tomorrow I'll be all alone here. *(She sighs)*

First, I'll give orders to chop down this row of pine trees, then the maple. At night, it looks really scary and really ugly.

(To Irina) My dear, that belt doesn't suit your face. It's the height of bad tastefulness. You need a pastel. And I'll order little flowers to be planted . . . everywhere, little flowers! And they'll make so much smell! *(Suddenly stern)* Why is there a fork here lying on a swing?

(Crossing into the house, shouting) Why is there a fork lying on a swing, I'm talking to you!

(Screaming at the maid) Don't talk to me! Shut up!

KULYGIN

. . . And she's off—

The band plays a march. Everyone listens.

OLGA

They're leaving.

Chebutykin enters.

MASHA

All our boys are leaving. Well . . . happy journey.
(To Kulygin) Let's go home . . . Where are my hat and coat?

KULYGIN

I took them in the house . . . I'll go grab them, right away.

OLGA

Yes, let's all go home. It's time.

CHEBUTYKIN

Olga Sergeyevna!

OLGA

What?
What?

CHEBUTYKIN

Nothing . . . don't know how to say this . . .

He whispers in her ear.

OLGA

Not possible!

CHEBUTYKIN

Yes . . . that's the story . . . I'm exhausted, I've had it, can't talk.
Incidentally, it's all the same.

MASHA

What happened?

Olga embraces Irina.

OLGA

Terrible day, today . . .
I don't know how to tell you . . .

IRINA

What? Out with it. What? For God's sake! *(Crying)*

CHEBUTYKIN

The Baron was just killed in a duel.

IRINA

(Weeping quietly) I knew, I knew . . .

CHEBUTYKIN

(Sitting on a bench) I'm exhausted.
(Takes a newspaper out of his pocket)
Let them cry a little . . .
Tararaboomdeyay—think I'll sit down de-yay . . .
Isn't it all the same . . .

The three sisters stand with their arms around one another.

MASHA

Oh, the music!
They're leaving us, and one left absolutely and forever.
We're left alone to begin our lives over again.
We must live . . . we must live . . .

IRINA

(Putting her head on Olga's breast) One day the time will come
when we know why we suffer,
there will be an end to all this mystery—
but meanwhile we must live,
we must work, only work!
Tomorrow I'm going away, alone,
I'll teach school, and I'll give my life away
to the people who need it.
It's fall now;

winter will be here soon and cover the world with snow . . .
and I'll work, I will work . . .

OLGA

(Embracing both her sisters) The music is so happy, so brave, it
makes you want to *live!*
Oh, God!
Time will pass and we'll be gone forever, we'll be forgotten,
They will forget our faces, our voices, how many of us there were—
but our suffering will turn into joy for those living after us.
There will be happiness, peace—on this earth,
and they will remember us later with a gentle word—
they will bless us,
we who live now.
Oh, my sisters, our life isn't over yet.
We will live!
The music is so happy, so full of joy,
as if we're only one moment away from knowing
why we live, why we suffer . . .
Oh to know, only to know!

The music still plays, more and more softly.
Kulygin, smiling, happy, brings Masha's hat and coat.
Andrei pushes Bobik in his carriage.

CHEBUTYKIN

(Singing softly) Tararaboomdeay—think I'll sit down de-aye—
(Reading his newspaper)
It's all the same, all the same!

OLGA

To know, to know!

CURTAIN

Orlando

By Virginia Woolf
Adapted by Sarah Ruhl

For Polly Noonan

Production History

Orlando received its world premiere at Piven Theatre Workshop (Byrne and Joyce Piven, Co-Founders; Joyce Piven, Artistic Director Emeritus) in Evanston, Illinois, in 1998. It was directed by Joyce Piven; the set design was by Jack Magaw, the costume design was by Beth Tallon, the lighting design was by Byrne Piven, the sound design was by Joseph Fosco, the music was composed by Shira Piven; and the production stage manager was Wendy Walshe. The cast was:

ORLANDO	Scot Morton
ORLANDO	Justine Scarpa
SASHA/SINGER	Gita Tanner
QUEEN ELIZABETH	Polly Noonan
ARCHDUKE	David Barack
ARCHDUCHESS/EUPHROSYNE	Susan Ferrara
POET/SINGER/SHELMERDINE	Jonathan Clark
PENELOPE/FAVILLA	Erin Higgins
OTHELLO/CAPTAIN	Anthony Fleming III
DESDEMONA/CLORINDA	Joanne Underwood

Orlando opened at The Actors' Gang (Tim Robbins, Artistic Director; Greg Reiner, Managing Director) in Los Angeles in March 2003. It was directed by Joyce Piven; the set design was by Danila Korogodsky, the costume design was by Ann Closs-Farley, the lighting design was by Adam Greene, the sound design was by David Robbins; the choreography was by Lindsley Allen; and the stage manager was Erica R. Christensen. The cast was:

ORLANDO	Polly Noonan
SASHA/CHORUS	Yasuko Takahara
QUEEN ELIZABETH/CHORUS	Kate Walsh
ARCHDUKE/ARCHDUCHESS/CHORUS	Corey Lovett
FAVILLA/GRIMSDITCH/CHORUS	Lolly Ward
CLORINDA/CHORUS	Melanie Lora
EUPHROSYNE/DUPPER/CHORUS	Carmella Mulvihill
OTHELLO/SEA CAPTAIN/CHORUS	Nick Gillie,
	William James Jones
MARMADUKE/CHORUS	Alessandro Mastrobuono
SALESPERSON/CHORUS	Caleb Moody
THE POET/CHORUS	Nathan Kornelis

Orlando received a developmental reading at New Dramatists (Todd London, Artistic Director; Joel K. Ruark, Executive Director) in New York on July 1, 2010. The project received support from the Creativity Fund, a program made possible by a lead grant from the Andrew W. Mellon Foundation. It was directed by Rebecca Taichman; the sound design was by Ryan Rumery; the choreography was by Annie-B Parson; and the stage manager was Joan H. Cappello. The cast was:

ORLANDO	Cynthia Nixon
SASHA/DANCER	Sonja Kostich
SASHA/CHORUS	Natalie Gold
QUEEN ELIZABETH/CHORUS 1	David Greenspan
OTHELLO/CHORUS 2	Danyon Davis
MARMADUKE/CHORUS 3	Stephen Barker Turner
SAILOR/DANCER/CHORUS 4	David Neumann

Orlando received its New York premiere at Classic Stage Company (Brian Kulick, Artistic Director; Jessica R. Jenen, Executive Director) on September 23, 2010. It was directed by Rebecca

Taichman; the set design was by Allen Moyer, the costume design was by Anita Yavich, the lighting design was by Christopher Akerlind, the sound design and original music were by Christian Frederickson and Ryan Rumery; the choreography was by Annie-B Parson; and the production stage manager was Erin Maureen Koster. The cast was:

ORLANDO	Francesca Faridany
SASHA	Annika Boras
CHORUS	David Greenspan, Tom Nelis, Howard Overshown

Orlando opened at the Court Theatre (Charles Newell, Artistic Director; Stephen J. Albert, Executive Director) in Chicago on March 10, 2011. It was directed by Jessica Thebus; the set design was by Collette Pollard, the costume design was by Linda Roethke, the lighting design was by Jaymi Lee Smith, the sound design was by Andre Pluess; the dramaturg was Drew Dir and the stage manager was Erica R. Christensen. The cast was:

ORLANDO	Amy J. Carle
SASHA	Erica Elam
CHORUS	Amy J. Carle, Thomas J. Cox, Adrian Danzig, Kevin Douglass, Lawrence Grimm

CHARACTERS

ORLANDO *(played by a woman)*
SASHA *(played by a woman)*

THE CHORUS

(may be cast without regard to gender
may be double-cast
may be played by as few as three actors and as many as eight,
but the author suggests a chorus of three gifted men to play all the roles)

QUEEN ELIZABETH

SHAKESPEARE

THE ARCHDUKE/ARCHDUCHESS

MISS PENELOPE HARTROPP

A WASHERWOMAN

FAVILLA

CLORINDA

EUPHROSYNE

A RUSSIAN SEA MAN

OTHELLO

DESDEMONA

A SEA CAPTAIN

A MAID——GRIMSDITCH

A MAID——DUPPER

MARMADUKE BONTHROP SHELMERDINE, ESQUIRE

A SALESPERSON

ELEVATOR MAN

Notes on Orlando

On Scenic Design

I have seen this play designed many ways; on a plot of grass with a small golden replica of Knole; on something of a dangerous playground; on an open space with costume racks. The design is left purposely open.

On Costumes

The costumes must by necessity transform; otherwise you're stuck making dozens of costumes from too many literal periods. In one production, Queen Elizabeth's dress was a two-dimensional placard that flew down from the ceiling and was placed on David Greenspan's body. In another production, all the male chorus members wore white corsets. In any case, the scenic design and the costume design need to depend heavily on transformation, metaphor, emptiness and playfulness.

On Choral Speaking and Casting

The text is not broken down specifically into who says what, because each production will determine exactly who and what the chorus is, and how many members there are. I recommend extensively playing with who says what in the rehearsal room before setting it. The text is not designed to be spoken all at once by everyone, but instead to be worked at and worked at until the chorus appears to speak with one voice, although the text is broken up.

While I have seen large and small choruses, my favorite way to do this play is to have two women (one playing Orlando and one playing Sasha), surrounded by a chorus of three very gifted men, who play all the other roles. The reason I like this configuration is that it's the most economical and virtuosic, and performs gender seamlessly. However I can imagine all sorts of other configurations, and all sorts of large ensembles creating new structures for the play. I have also always wanted to do the play on alternating nights; on Mondays, have a man play Orlando (and a woman play Marmaduke), on Tuesdays, have a woman play Orlando (and a man play Marmaduke).

On Movement

It is difficult to imagine the New York production of *Orlando* without the choreography of the brilliant Annie-B Parson, or the first production without the circus artist Sylvia Hernandez-DiStasi and choreographer Toby Nicholson. The non-literal language of dance should work in counter-point to Woolf's surfeit of language. I wish I could describe to you the hand gestures Annie-B gave to Orlando when she was lost in contemplation, or the way Sasha rested her head in the palm of Orlando's hand; alas these gestures are lost in time, but you will find your own. The best choreographer I can imagine for *Orlando* is one who does not like "choreography."

On Narration

I wrote this play for Joyce Piven, who asked me to adapt *Orlando* when I was twenty-two, before I was too old to realize that it might be a difficult task. Because I wrote it for her and her company, I wrote it for an ensemble who was already well versed in using narration on stage. Some might call that mode story theater, but I think that compound word has been so misunderstood and maligned that I prefer to just call it narration. Actors understand intuitively how to narrate; we tell stories about our own behavior all the time "and then I said . . ." or "and then this guy walked in and he was wearing a blue shirt and he said . . . " It is a linguistic modality as old as language and a theater modality as old as the Greeks. But because of the dominant mode of naturalism, narration onstage has the power to flummox some actors and some audience members. Even some directors. My cardinal rules of narration are these:

1. Simplicity. When in doubt make a simple choice.
2. Emotional statedness. There is an emotional undercurrent in narration; it is not the neutral tone that "a narrator" in a children's play would adopt.
3. Non-literalness or non-illustration. The actor need not always do the thing he or she is doing; the gesture need not illustrate the narration precisely.
4. Flux. The nature of the narration will change, moment to moment. It needn't have static rules to guide it.
5. The audience. The story is always for the audience. They are always there. The narration invites them in rather than distancing them.

I have always enjoyed this passage about Vietnamese Ceo theater, and it reminds me of the kind of story theater I grew up on:

In the Russian tradition of Stanislavsky, the actor says, "I will tell you a story about me." In the German tradition of Brecht, the actor says, "I will tell you a story about them." In the Vietnamese tradition, the actor says, "You and I will tell each other a story about all of us."

—"In Vietnam, Telling Stories About 'All of Us,'"
Ron Jenkins, *New York Times*, August 11, 2002"

The reason I used a great deal of narration in this piece is that Woolf's language is so much better than any of her imitators could ever be; and all the narration in the piece is hers and hers alone.

A Note on Vita and Virginia

Called "the longest love letter in the history of English letters" by Vita Sackville-West's son, Virginia Woolf wrote *Orlando* for her great love Vita, and she wrote it more quickly (and more happily) than any other novel. Orlando is, then, a composite of Vita and her many lives, and getting a good annotated copy of *Orlando* will help a production find its way into the specificity and intimacy of the novel's original intent. I recommend the Penguin 1993 edition, annotated by Sandra M. Gilbert.

Act I: The Elizabethan Age

Scene 1: Orlando

CHORUS

The age was Elizabethan.
Their morals were not ours.
Nor their poets, nor their climate
nor their vegetables even.
Everything was different.
The rain fell vehemently or not at all.
The sun blazed or there was darkness.
Violence was all.

And, standing next to a large oak tree,
was a boy, called
Orlando.

Orlando jumps on a chair.

ORLANDO

HE—

CHORUS

HE!

ORLANDO

(To the audience—a conspiracy) He—for there could be no doubt
of his sex . . .

CHORUS

Though the fashion of the age did something to disguise it—

Orlando raises his sword and swings it.

CHORUS

Was in the act of slicing at the head of an infidel!

Orlando looks at the audience. "He" is surprised and a bit crestfallen.
Orlando is constantly surprising him/herself in the act of performance.

ORLANDO

I do so long to chop the head off an infidel,
but I am, as yet, only sixteen.

Orlando looks into a mirror.

CHORUS

Sights exulted him—
the birds and the trees—

ORLANDO

and made him in love with death . . .

Orlando looks at the chorus. They disperse.

ORLANDO

I am alone.

CHORUS

He sighed profoundly.

Orlando sighs profoundly.

CHORUS

And flung himself
on the earth
at the foot of
the oak tree.

Orlando flings himself down in front of an oak tree.

ORLANDO

And in his mind, image followed image:

CHORUS

The oak tree was
the back of a great horse
that he was riding

or

the deck of a tumbling ship

it was anything indeed
so long as it was hard

ORLANDO

for he felt the need of something
which he could attach
his floating heart to.

I will—

CHORUS

Orlando thought—

ORLANDO

I will write a great poem
about the Oak Tree.

CHORUS

And he tried to describe—
For all young poets are forever describing—
Nature.

ORLANDO

He wanted to match the shade of green
Precisely—

The green of the grass, the green of the grass . . .
The greeny greeny green of the grass—

CHORUS

But green in nature is one thing
Green in literature quite another.

When—
(A trumpet sound)
A Trumpet Sounded!!!

ORLANDO

Tomorrow.
I will write a great poem
About the oak tree tomorrow.

More trumpets.
Orlando leaps to his feet.

ORLANDO

Orlando saw that his great house—
in the valley—
was pierced with lights.

CHORUS

Coaches turned and wheeled.
Horses tossed their plumes.

And why did horses toss their plumes?

ORLANDO

Christ Jesus!

ORLANDO AND CHORUS

THE QUEEN HAD COME.

CHORUS

Orlando dashed downhill.

The chorus dresses Orlando.

CHORUS

He let himself in at a wicket gate.
He tore up the winding staircase.
He tripped.
(He was a trifle clumsy.)
He reached his room.
He scoured his hands.
He pared his fingernails.
With no more than six inches of
looking-glass and a pair of old candles
to help him, he had thrust on
crimson breeches
a lace collar
and shoes
with rosettes
as big as
double
dahlias.

He was ready.
He was flushed.
He was excited.

ORLANDO

But he was terribly late.

143

He reached the banqueting hall only just in time
to sink upon his knees and, hanging his head in confusion,
to offer a bowl of rose water to the . . .

ORLANDO AND CHORUS

great
Queen
herself.

Scene 2: The Queen

The Queen extends her hand.
Orlando kneels before her.

ORLANDO
Such was Orlando's shyness that he saw no
more of her than her ringed hand in water, but
it was enough.

ORLANDO AND CHORUS
It was a memorable hand.

THE QUEEN
A thin hand with long fingers always curling as if 'round orb or
scepter;

ORLANDO
a nervous, crabbed, sickly hand;

THE QUEEN

a commanding hand, a hand that had only to raise itself for a head to fall; yes, the Queen had a hand—

ORLANDO

—Orlando guessed, attached to an old body that smelt like a cupboard.

THE QUEEN

Come.

Orlando approaches the Queen and kneels at her feet.

THE QUEEN

The Queen studied Orlando.
She read him like a page—Eyes, mouth, nose, hips, hands . . .
By God! He has the shapeliest legs of any nobleman in England!

ORLANDO

He only felt something press against his hair . . .

The Queen kisses Orlando's hair.

CHORUS

He had been kissed by a queen without knowing it.

THE QUEEN

What is your name, dear boy?

ORLANDO

Orlando.

THE QUEEN

Orlando! And what do you want to be when you grow up, Orlando?

ORLANDO

I would very much like to be a poet, Your Highness.

THE QUEEN

Ah, romance, folly, poetry, youth! I think you would make a fine poet, Orlando. And I have always wanted a gentleman just your age. How would you like to come to Court, Orlando?

ORLANDO

To Court—that's a very great honor, Your Highness.

THE QUEEN

Yes.

The Queen plucked a ring from her finger—
The joint was rather swollen—

Orlando, I want to give you this ring. I hereby name you my Treasurer and Steward.

ORLANDO

Thank you, Mum.

CHORUS

And the Queen took Orlando to Court.

THE QUEEN

For the old woman loved Orlando.

CHORUS

Lands were given him
A great house assigned him.

THE QUEEN

He was to be the son of her old age.

CHORUS

And the flower bloomed and faded.
And the sun rose and sank.

The Queen leads Orlando to her bedroom and pulls him down among the cushions.

THE QUEEN

I hope that you will stay with me always.

ORLANDO

Yes, Mum.

CHORUS

And the flower bloomed and faded.
And the sun rose and sank.

THE QUEEN

Shall we play a game, Orlando?

ORLANDO

Yes, Mum. What is the game?

THE QUEEN

First you recite a Petrarchan sonnet on my eyes,
and then I challenge you to an ode upon my feet.

ORLANDO

Yes, Mum.

THE QUEEN

And if they are very good, you may kiss me.

ORLANDO

Yes, Mum.

Shall I compare thee to a summer's day?
Thou art more lovely and more temperate . . .

THE QUEEN

That's enough, Orlando. I believe I've heard that one before. But
it was very, very good, and you may kiss me.

She kisses him, passionately.

148

THE QUEEN

This—

CHORUS

The Queen breathed—

THE QUEEN

Is my victory!

CHORUS

And the flower bloomed and faded.
And the sun rose and sank.

Orlando sighs.

THE QUEEN

What *is* the matter, Orlando?

ORLANDO

Mum?

THE QUEEN

Are you quite content? You don't seem your usual self. Did you
enjoy the parakeets from the Azores?

ORLANDO

Very much, Mum.

THE QUEEN

Perhaps you are bored. Perhaps you do not play with boys your
own age quite enough.

ORLANDO

How could boys my own age compare with a queen, Mum?

THE QUEEN

That's the spirit, Orlando.

Scene 3: Man's Treachery

CHORUS

The long winter months drew on.

ORLANDO

Frost covered all the trees—

THE QUEEN

And the nights were of perfect stillness.

CHORUS

One morning . . .

THE QUEEN

The Queen was getting dressed.

CHORUS

(Dressing the Queen) Your stockings, Mum—
Your farthingdale, Mum—

which was tightened
and fastened—

THE QUEEN

Not too tight!

CHORUS

until the Queen floated
as if on her own island.

THE QUEEN

She powdered her face.

CHORUS

She was practicing a speech.

THE QUEEN

My loving people. I know I have the body but of a weak and
feeble woman, but I have the heart and stomach of a king, and of
a King of England too—

ORLANDO

When all of a sudden—

THE QUEEN

the Queen saw in the mirror . . .

CHORUS

which she kept for fear of spies . . .

THE QUEEN

through the door . . .
a boy . . .

ORLANDO

Could it be Orlando?

THE QUEEN

kissing a girl—
Who in the devil's name *is* that brazen hussy?
Snatching at her golden sword she struck violently at the mirror.

CHORUS

The glass crashed.
People came running.
She was lifted and set in her chair again.
But she was stricken after that
and groaned for many years:

THE QUEEN

Man's treachery.

CHORUS

It was Orlando's fault, perhaps.

ORLANDO

Yet, after all, are we to blame Orlando?
He was young, he was boyish.
He did as nature bade him do.

CLORINDA, FAVILLA AND EUPHROSYNE

It is certain indeed that many
ladies were ready to show him their favors.

They giggle.

Scene 4: Orlando Grows Tired of the Queen
Or: Clorinda, Favilla and Euphrosyne

FAVILLA

Favilla's grace in dancing had won the admiration of all.

EUPHROSYNE

The second, Euphrosyne, was by far the most serious of Orlando's flames.

CLORINDA

And the third, Clorinda, could not bear the sight of blood, and the smell of roast meat made her faint. She took it upon herself to reform Orlando.

ORLANDO

Orlando did not much regret it when Clorinda died soon after of the small-pox.

Clorinda falls dead to the floor. Favilla and Euphrosyne look at her,
not a little pleased.

FAVILLA

Once, however, Favilla was so ill-advised as to whip a spaniel—that
had torn one of her silk stockings—beneath Orlando's window.

ORLANDO

I love animals.

FAVILLA

Oh . . .

ORLANDO

Orlando now noticed that her teeth were crooked, which is a sure
sign of a perverse and cruel disposition in a woman.

I'm sorry, but I'm forced to break off our engagement forever.

Favilla exits, lips trembling.

EUPHROSYNE

Euphrosyne sang in Italian well—
(A snatch of a song in Italian)
And she was never without a spaniel.
She fed them white bread from her own plate—
(To an imaginary spaniel, in Italian)
Come here my darling . . .

Euphrosyne would have made a perfect wife for a nobleman such
as Orlando—

ORLANDO

I will have my lawyers draw up the settlements, darling.

Orlando kissed Euphrosyne on her serious white cheek.

CHORUS

When, with suddenness and severity, came
The
Great
Frost.

Scene 5: The Great Frost. The Russian Princess.

Sounds of wind and skates scraping against ice.

CHORUS
Birds froze in mid-air
and fell like stones to the ground.

It was no uncommon sight to come upon
a whole herd of swine frozen immovable upon the road.

The fields were full of shepherds all struck stark
in the act of the moment
one with his hand to his nose
another with the bottle to his lips
a third with a stone raised to throw at
a raven who sat, as if stuffed, upon the hedge.

But while the country people suffered,
London enjoyed a carnival
of the utmost brilliancy.

Music and trumpets.
Flowers fall from the sky.
A Great Spectacle.

CHORUS

Frozen roses fell in showers when the Queen and her courtiers
walked abroad.
Colored balloons hovered motionless in the air.
Lovers dallied upon divans.
The ice went so deep and so clear that there could be seen,
congealed at a depth of a few thousand feet,
here a porpoise,
there a flounder!!!

ORLANDO

Orlando was gazing at a frozen flounder five fathoms beneath the
frozen sea . . .

An androgynous, captivating figure—Sasha—skates by in slow motion,
circling Orlando.

SASHA

(In a Russian accent) When a figure skated by him . . .

CHORUS

Orlando, upon seeing the figure, shouted in his own mind,

ORLANDO

(Shouting at the girl) melon, pineapple, olive tree, emerald, fox in
the snow—

CHORUS

All in the space of three seconds.
He did not know whether he had heard her,
tasted her,
seen her,
or all three together.

And then *the boy* skated by—
for alas, Orlando,
a boy it must be.

Orlando looks at the chorus—incredulous.

CHORUS

Legs, hands, and carriage, were a boy's.
No woman could skate with such speed and vigor.

ORLANDO

(To the audience) Orlando was ready to tear his hair with vexation
that this fine person was of his own sex.

He asks the Queen:

ORLANDO

All embraces are out of the question?

The Queen nods.

SASHA

(In a Russian accent) But no boy ever had a mouth like that—

CHORUS

no boy had those breasts—

ORLANDO

no boy had eyes which looked
as if they had been fished from the bottom
of the sea.

SASHA

The unknown skater came to a standstill.

ORLANDO AND CHORUS

SHE WAS A WOMAN.

Cheering.
Sasha speaks Russian to Orlando, something ending in "Marousha
Stanilovska Dagmar Natasha Iliana Romanovitch."

SASHA

(To the audience) A translation. Hello. I am the Princess Marousha Stanilovska Dagmar Natasha Iliana Romanovitch.

ORLANDO

Orlando trembled, turned hot, turned cold, longed to crush acorns
beneath his feet.

(To Sasha)
Will you come to dinner?

SASHA

Parlez-vous français?

ORLANDO

(Amorously) Oui.

They go off, arm in arm.
They sit at a grand banquet table with many nobles.
Sasha laughs and chatters in French.
Orlando is dumbstruck.

ORLANDO

(To the audience) Whom had he loved, what had he loved, until
now? An old woman, all skin and bone. A nodding mass of lace
and ceremony.

Watching the Princess, the thickness of his blood melted. The
ice turned to wine in his veins. His manhood woke; he grasped a
sword in his hand; he charged . . .

Sasha speaks gibberish French to Orlando; it sounds like a sexual
invitation.

SASHA

(To the audience) A translation. Would you have the goodness to
pass the salt?

*Orlando speaks gibberish French to Sasha; it sounds like a sexual
invitation.*

ORLANDO

(To the audience) A translation. With all the pleasure in the world,
madam.

He passes her the salt.
Sasha speaks to Orlando in gibberish French,
putting her hand on his knee.
Orlando looks at her, bewitched.

CHORUS

A translation.
Who are these bumpkins?
Does the Duke always slobber like that?
Is the figure with her hair like a maypole really the Queen?

THE QUEEN

Thus began an intimacy between the two which soon became the
scandal of the Court.

The Queen gets up and slams down her chair.
Everyone gasps.
Orlando and the Princess do not notice.

Scene 6: *Orlando and Sasha*

CHORUS

In one night, Orlando had thrown off his boyish clumsiness and become a nobleman.

Everywhere one went, one saw Orlando handing Sasha—
the Russian Princess—to her sledge—

ORLANDO

Your sledge, madam.

CHORUS

or catching the spotted kerchief which she had let drop.

Sasha walks by dropping a kerchief. Orlando picks it up.

ORLANDO

Your handkerchief . . .

EUPHROSYNE

(To audience) Everyone knew that Orlando was engaged to another—

(To a friend)
Me!
I wear his sapphire on my left hand.

(To the audience)
Yet Euphrosyne might drop all the handkerchiefs in her wardrobe upon the ice and Orlando never stooped to pick them up.

Euphrosyne drops a profusion of handkerchiefs on the ground.

EUPHROSYNE

Orlando! Orlando! I've dropped my handkerchief! Orlando!

Orlando and Sasha don't notice her.

CHORUS

But what most outraged the Court
was that the couple was often seen to slip
under the silken rope
which railed off the Royal enclosure
from the common people.

Sasha and Orlando slip under the rope.

SASHA

Take me away. I detest your English Court. It is full of prying old women. They smell bad. It is like being in cage. In Russia we have rivers ten miles broad on which one can gallop all day without meeting a soul. I want to leave the Court!

ORLANDO

Do you fancy seeing London?

SASHA

I don't know—what is in this London?

ORLANDO

The Tower, the Beefeaters, the jeweler's shops, the theaters . . .

SASHA

Ah! Yes. I would like to see your London.

ORLANDO AND SASHA

So they skated to London on the frozen Thames.
They got further and further away from Court.

The sound of skates scraping against ice.

ORLANDO

Hot with skating . . .

SASHA

And with love . . .

ORLANDO

They would throw themselves down on a solitary place . . .

SASHA

Wrapped in a great fur cloak . . .

ORLANDO

Orlando would take her in his arms and know . . .

SASHA

For the first time . . .

ORLANDO

The delights of love.

They kiss, wrapped in a great fur cloak.

SASHA

Then, they would speak of everything under the sun.

ORLANDO

For instance:

SASHA

This man's beard!

ORLANDO

That woman's skin!

SASHA

A rat that fed from my hand!

ORLANDO

A face!

SASHA

A feather!

ORLANDO

Nothing was too small for such talk.

SASHA

Nothing was too great.
Sometimes Orlando would be melancholy.

ORLANDO

All ends in death.

SASHA

But I do not like Orlando to be melancholy. So I speak to him
enchantingly, wittily, wisely (but always in French, which I'm
afraid loses its flavor in translation).

She whispers French into his ear.

ORLANDO

You are a fox, an olive tree, an emerald.

Orlando tried to tell her what she was like—
Darling, you are a—a—

but words failed him.

He wanted another landscape, and another tongue. English was
too frank for describing Sasha. In all that the Princess said, there
was something hidden.

SASHA

(To the audience) What did she hide from him?

She touches his cheek and smiles mysteriously.

SASHA

(To Orlando) One day we will live in Russia together, where there
are frozen rivers and wild horses and men who gash each other's
throats open.

ORLANDO

(To Sasha) Yes, my love.

(To the audience)
But habits of lust and slaughter did not entice him.

Orlando pulls Sasha up and they begin skating again.
The sound of skates scraping against ice.

CHORUS

One day, after skating for twenty hours,
they reached a part of the river
where ships had anchored and been frozen.
Among them was the ship of the Russian Embassy.

The sound of a Russian sea-song sung by sea men.

SASHA

Greetings, countrymen!

Her countrymen greet her in Russian. She goes aboard the ship.

CENTER SASHA

(To Orlando) I'll be back soon, my love! Wait for me! I only want
to say hello to my countrymen!

ORLANDO

Don't be long, darling!

CHORUS

So Orlando waited.
He walked up and down the ice.

ORLANDO

He thought only of the pleasures of life.

CHORUS

The sun was sinking rapidly.

ORLANDO

Still, he waited.
Sasha had been gone an hour.

The sound of a bell tolling the hour.

ORLANDO

Orlando was seized with dark forebodings.
He could wait no longer.

CHORUS

He dashed into the ship.

*Orlando opens a door to the ship. Inside the ship, Orlando freezes.
He sees Sasha on a sailor's knee.
She bends toward the sailor in slow motion, embracing him.*

CHORUS

Orlando blazed into such a howl of anguish that the
WHOLE SHIP ECHOED!!!

Orlando leaps at the sailor, Sasha throws herself between them.

Orlando collapses. Sasha revives him.

SASHA

Orlando, dear, are you all right? What is the matter? You must have been dreaming. You must have been faint!

ORLANDO

You—you bent towards a sailor—you kissed him.

SASHA

The room was dark—shadows must have moved. There was a heavy box, I helped one of my countrymen to move it.

ORLANDO

You did?

SASHA

Yes.

ORLANDO

It *was* very dark in the room.

SASHA

Yes, it was very, very dark.

ORLANDO

Yes. Kiss me and forgive me my folly.

They kiss.

ORLANDO

No! I saw you! You kissed him! You did! You did!

SASHA

I call upon the gods to destroy me if I, a Royal Romanovitch, laid in the arms of a common sea man!

I will leave this very night.

ORLANDO

Orlando looked at the sailor.

SEA MAN

(*With Russian accent*) The man was huge, wore common wire
rings in his ears, and looked like a horse upon which a robin had
perched in its flight.

The sea man winds heavy rope in his hands and looks at Orlando.
Orlando looks at Sasha.
Orlando looks at the sea man.
Orlando looks at Sasha.

SASHA

Well?

ORLANDO

Don't leave me, Sasha. You must forgive me. If I am a jealous
fool, it is only because I love you.

SASHA

I forgive you this time. But you must never again doubt me, Orlando.

They link arms.

SASHA AND ORLANDO

And so they skated again towards London,
arm in arm.

ORLANDO

Suspicions melted in his breast, and he felt as if he had been
hooked by a great fish through the nose and rushed through the
waters unwillingly, yet with his own consent.

Scene 7: London

The sound of skates scraping against ice.

CHORUS
It was an evening of astonishing beauty.
The domes, spires, turrets and pinnacles of London rose in blackness
against furious clouds.

ORLANDO AND SASHA
They sped quicker and quicker to the city.

SASHA
I used to listen to the wolves howling in Russia in the winter—
they sounded like this— *(She howls)*

Orlando swings her around.

ORLANDO
And he swung her across the rivers so that the gulls swung too.

SASHA

Orlando—I feel compelled to tell you—I love you for your love
of beasts. And for your gallantry. And for your legs.

ORLANDO

I can find no words to praise you, Sasha.

SASHA

You are like a million-candled Christmas tree such as we have in
Russia—enough to light a whole street by.

CHORUS

And indeed, he looked as if he were burning with his own
radiance, from a lamp lit within.

ORLANDO

Night came on.

SASHA AND ORLANDO

The Royal Couple found themselves in the midst of the common
people—

CHORUS

A Carnival!!!
All the riff-raff of London was there
Here throwing dice
There telling fortunes
Shoving
tickling
pinching,
all
pressing forward
towards a
stage.

The chorus whistles, boos, stamps its feet.
They come upon a performance of Othello.

ORLANDO

Shall we stop and look, Sasha?

SASHA

Oh, please, let's watch—we haven't such things in Russia.

ORLANDO

You don't mind sitting so close to the commoners?

SASHA

Oh, no, they smell much better than your Queen.

Orlando takes Sasha's hands, enraptured.

OTHELLO

That handkerchief which I so love and gave thee
Thou gav'st to Cassio.

DESDEMONA

No, by my life and soul!
Send for the man and ask him.

OTHELLO

Sweet soul, take heed,
Take heed of perjury; thou art on thy deathbed.

DESDEMONA

Ay, but not yet to die.

OTHELLO

Yes, presently.

ORLANDO

The melody of the words stirred Orlando like music.

DESDEMONA

I never did
Offend you in my life; never loved Cassio

171

But with such general warranty of heaven
As I might love. I never gave him token.

OTHELLO

By heaven, I saw my handkerchief in's hand!
O perjured woman! thou dost stone my heart—

DESDEMONA

O banish me, my lord, but kill me not!
Kill me tomorrow, let me live tonight!

OTHELLO

Nay if you strive—

DESDEMONA

But half an hour? But while I say one prayer!

OTHELLO

It is too late.

Othello smothers her.
Othello stabs himself and falls over Desdemona.
The audience sighs, groans, boos, applauds, and throws things.

ORLANDO

Tears streamed down Orlando's face.
The frenzy of the Moor seemed to him his own frenzy.
It was Sasha he killed with his own two hands.

Ruin and death—Orlando thought—
cover all.

SASHA

Orlando—do you remember—
It was on a night such as this—dark and cold—

ORLANDO

We planned to escape—to leave Court—

SASHA

To elope.

ORLANDO

The time has come.

ORLANDO AND SASHA

Jour de ma vie!

CHORUS

It was their signal.

ORLANDO

Meet me at Blackfriars, at the inn, at midnight. Horses will be waiting for us.

CHORUS

Blackfriars.

They part with a kiss.

Scene 8: The Escape

Orlando paces at Blackfriars. The light sound of rain.

ORLANDO

Long before midnight, Orlando was waiting.
He checked his things: money, food, wine, compass . . .
Sasha, where is Sasha?

CHORUS

Sometimes, in the darkness, he seemed to see her
wrapped about with rain strokes.
But still, she did not come.

ORLANDO

Suddenly, he was struck in the face by a blow,
soft, yet heavy, on his cheek.

Who is there?

174

He put his hand to his sword.
The frost had lasted so long that it
took him a minute to realize that these
were raindrops falling.

The heavier sound of rain.

CHORUS

Soon the six drops became sixty
then six hundred.

ORLANDO

Sasha!

CHORUS

The water rose.
Ice cracked off the trees.

ORLANDO

Sasha!
He would wait, he would wait . . .

CHORUS

Suddenly, with an ominous voice,
St. Paul's struck the first stroke
of midnight.

The clock continues to toll. The sound of rain.

ORLANDO

Sasha!
She will come on the sixth stroke, she will come on the sixth
stroke, she will come on the sixth stroke . . .

*The sixth stroke. Other clocks begin to sound the hour, jangling one
after the other—cuckoo clocks, alarm clocks, bells . . .*

CHORUS

The whole world seemed to ring with the news of her deceit.
Through the rain,
he could just make out the shape of a ship
on the horizon, moving through icebergs.

ORLANDO

The ship of the Russian Embassy!

Sasha appears on the prow of a ship.

ORLANDO

Sasha!
Sasha!
Sasha!
Sasha!

CHORUS

And then: silence.
The waters took his words,
and tossed at his feet only a broken pot
and a bit of straw.

Act II: The Seventeenth Century

Scene 1: The Thaw. Also, the Archduchess.

ORLANDO

I am alone.

CHORUS

The dawn broke with unusual suddenness,
and a sight of the most extraordinary nature met Orlando's eyes.

ORLANDO

Where there had once been solid ice
was now a race of turbulent yellow waters.

CHORUS

All was riot and confusion.
The river was strewn with icebergs.

ORLANDO

What was most terrible was the sight of
the human creatures, trapped on the ice.

CHORUS	A YOUNG WOMAN
Some cried out and	*(An improvised*
made wild promises to God.	*wild promise to God)*

CHORUS
Others were dazed with terror,
looking steadfastly before them.

CHORUS	
Others called for vengeance:	AN OLD MAN
	Vengence upon
	the dirty Irish rebels!

	AN OLD WOMAN
Some perished clasping a silver pot	My teapot! My teapot!
or other treasure to their breasts.	

Among other strange sights
to be seen was a table laid sumptuously
for twenty on an iceberg.

ORLANDO
Or a couple in bed
together with an extraordinary number of cooking utensils.

Orlando gazed, astounded.

CHORUS
But, seeming to recollect himself,
he galloped hard along the river bank,
until he reached his great house in the country.

ORLANDO
(To the audience) Orlando now took a strange delight in thoughts
of death and decay.

(To the chorus)
Are we so made that we have to take death in small doses daily or
we could not go on with the business of living?

(To the gods)
I am done with women!

CHORUS

He stood shaken with sobs, all for the desire of a woman in Russian trousers—

ORLANDO

Faithless, fickle, devil, adultress, wench . . .

I must do something. I must do something. I must write.

CHORUS

Orlando would have given every penny to write one little book and become famous—and yet, all the gold in Peru would not buy him the treasure of one well-turned line . . .

ORLANDO

Fame is like . . . a braided coat which hampers the limbs, a jacket of silver which curbs the heart . . . Confound it all! Why not simply say what one means!

Orlando throws himself at the foot of the oak tree.

CHORUS

One day, he was adding a line or two with enormous labor to "The Oak Tree, A Poem"—

ORLANDO

The grass is green . . . and the sky is . . . blue . . .

CHORUS

When a shadow crossed the edge of his paper.

The Archduchess—a man in drag—approaches.

ORLANDO

It was no shadow—
but a very tall lady in riding hood and mantle.

ARCHDUCHESS

(Tee-hee's need not be taken literally)
Forgive my intrusion. (Tee-hee.) (Haw-haw.)

ORLANDO

She spoke with so much tee-heeing and haw-hawing that Orlando
thought she must have escaped from a lunatic asylum.

ARCHDUCHESS

I am the Archduchess Harriet Griselda of Finster-Aarhorn Scand-
Op Boom in the Romanian territory. (Tee-hee.) I desire above all
things to make your acquaintance. (Haw-haw.) I saw your picture
and it was the image of a sister of mine who was— (Haw-haw.)
—long since dead. I'm visiting the English Court, the Queen
being my cousin. (Tee-hee.) (Haw-haw.)

ORLANDO

I see.

ARCHDUCHESS

Well— (Tee-hee.) —don't good manners require you to ask me
in and offer me a glass of wine? (Haw-haw.)

ORLANDO

Certainly. This way.

ARCHDUCHESS

Everything they say is true! You have the shapeliest legs that any
nobleman has ever stood upon!

ORLANDO

Thank you.

ARCHDUCHESS

Oh my! (Tee-hee.) Your ankle buckle is undone! Shall I clasp it
for you? I must!

ORLANDO

If you must.

The Archduchess leans down and fastens Orlando's shoe, rubbing her hands up and down his shin.

CHORUS

Orlando was violently overcome by a passion of some sort.

ORLANDO

Excuse me.

(To himself)
What sort of passion can this be?
It's unaccountable.

CHORUS

For when the Archduchess stooped
to fasten his buckle,
Orlando heard—

ORLANDO

far off, the beating of Love's wings—
He was ready to raise his hands and let the bird of beauty
alight upon his shoulders when—horror!

ARCHDUCHESS

Orlando!

CHORUS

A vulture landed on Orlando's shoulder.

ARCHDUCHESS

(Amorously) Orlando! I'm waiting!

ORLANDO

Just a moment!
Oh, God . . .

CHORUS

For love has two faces and two bodies—
one smooth,
the other hairy.

181

You see—it was not Love, the bird of Paradise—
who landed on Orlando's shoulder,
but Lust, the vulture.

ARCHDUCHESS
What's the matter, my innocent? (Tee-hee.) You seem flushed.
Has something excited you? (Haw-haw.)

ORLANDO
No, I'm quite all right, thank you.

ARCHDUCHESS
(Chasing him) Ooh! Your stockings have a little hole in them!
Shall I mend them?

CHORUS
And the Archduchess called on him the next day.

ARCHDUCHESS
Orlando.

CHORUS
And the next.

ARCHDUCHESS
Orlando.

CHORUS
And the next.

ARCHDUCHESS
Orlando!

ORLANDO
Orlando realized that his home was now uninhabitable.

CHORUS
So Orlando did what any other young man would have done in
his place. He asked the King . . .

Orlando kneels.

ORLANDO

Please, my Lord. Send me to Constantinople.

CHORUS

Constantinople.

Scene 2: Constantinople

Birds. Turkish music. Orlando is set upon a blanket.

CHORUS

In Constantinople, Orlando possessed
the power to stir the fancy and rivet the eye.
His power was a mysterious one, composed
of beauty, birth, and some rarer gift, which we may call—

AN AMOROUS PERSON FROM THE TABLEAU

Glamour!

CHORUS

And have done with it.

AN AMOROUS WOMAN FROM THE TABLEAU

He became the adored of many women—

AN AMOROUS MAN FROM THE TABLEAU

And some men.

ORLANDO

Could someone massage my temples?

The tableau competes to massage his temples.

CHORUS

And yet, this romantic power, it is well known,
is often associated with a nature of extreme shyness.
Orlando seems to have made no friends.

The amorous tableau turns away.

ORLANDO

So, one night, he threw a terrific party.

CHORUS

We happen to have here a letter from one Miss Penelope Hartropp,
who attended the party, addressed to her cousin in England:

PENELOPE HARTROPP

It was ravishing!
Utterly beyond description!
Swans made to represent water lilies!
Birds in golden cages!
And Orlando!
To see him come into the room!
To see him go out again!
Mr. Peregrine said I looked *quite* lovely
which I only repeat to you my dearest, because
I *know* you would want to know . . .

CHORUS

We also have, from the testimony of a washerwoman—

WASHERWOMAN

Who was kept awake by a headache—

CHORUS

A report that—

WASHERWOMAN

(Cockney accent) I saw a woman of the peasant class drawn up by a rope to Orlando's balcony. A Spanish dancer, I believe—*a gypsy*, named Rosina Pepita. There they embraced passionately—like lovers, see—and with that, they went into Orlando's bedroom and drew the curtains so that no more could be seen.

Orlando and his lady friend disappear behind the changing screen.

CHORUS

We only mention this event—
quite trivial in the long history
of Orlando's many affairs—
because, the next morning,
an extraordinary, and somewhat
inexplicable, event occurred.

The next morning,
though dogs were set to
bark under his window, still,
Orlando did not wake.

The sound of dogs, trumpets, drums.

CHORUS

Morning and evening, they tried to wake him,
but still Orlando slept.
On the sixth day of Orlando's trance,
the Turks rose against the Sultan,
set fire to the town,
and put foreigners to death.
Gentlemen of the British embassy
preferred to swallow bunches of keys
rather than fall into
the hands of the Infidel.
Still, Orlando slept.
On the seventh day,

he awoke.
He stretched himself.
He stood upright in complete
nakedness before us,
while the trumpets pealed out:
Truth!
Truth!
Truth!

Orlando stretches, naked, behind the screen. We see "his" silhouette.

CHORUS

We have no choice but to confess . . .
he was a woman.

The chorus looks at Orlando.

CHORUS

No human being, since the world began, has ever looked more
ravishing. His form combined in one the strength of a man and a
woman's grace.

Orlando emerges and looks at herself in a mirror.

CHORUS

And here we pause.
Orlando had become a woman—there is no denying it.
But in every other respect, Orlando remained precisely as he had
been.

Many people hold that such a change of sex is against nature and
have been at pains to prove, first, that Orlando had always been
a woman, and secondly, that Orlando is at this moment a man.
Let biologists and psychologists determine.
It is enough for us to state the simple fact:
Orlando was a man till the age of thirty, when he became a woman
and has remained so ever since.

ORLANDO

I want to go home.

To England.

The sound of water. Intermission.

Act III: The Eighteenth Century

Scene 1: Orlando Sails Back to England.

Orlando appears on the deck of a ship, wearing a huge, confining, elaborate dress and hat.
The sound of a boat rocking in water.

ORLANDO
Orlando bought herself a complete outfit of such clothes as women then wore, and it was in just such a dress that she now stood on the deck of a ship heading towards England. It is a strange fact, but a true one, that up to this moment she had scarcely given her sex a thought. It was not until she felt the coil of skirts about her legs and the captain offered—

CAPTAIN
May I get a chair for you, madam?

ORLANDO
Oh! Yes, please.
(Orlando rehearses the phrase "Yes, please" in varied tones, from "masculine" to "feminine") Yes, please.

The captain brings her a chair and she stretches out.

ORLANDO

At that moment, she realized with a start the penalties and privileges of her position.

This is a pleasant, lazy way of life to be sure. But could I leap overboard and swim in clothes like these? No!

CAPTAIN

Dinner?

ORLANDO

Yes, please.

The captain drops a napkin on her lap.

CAPTAIN

A little of the fat, madam? Let me cut you just the tiniest little slice the size of your fingernail.

ORLANDO

A delicious tremor ran through Orlando's frame.

CHORUS

Birds sang;
torrents rushed.

ORLANDO

She remembered the feeling of indescribable pleasure with which she had first seen Sasha, hundreds of years ago.

CAPTAIN

Madam?

ORLANDO

(To the captain) Well, if you wish it, I will have the very thinnest, smallest shiver of corned beef in the world.

CAPTAIN

Very good, madam.

ORLANDO

(To the audience) Nothing is more heavenly than to resist and to yield; to yield and to resist.

Orlando begins to eat, taking very small bites.

CHORUS

She was like a child entering into a toy cupboard;
her arguments would not commend themselves to mature women.

CAPTAIN

May I give you more sauce, madam?

Orlando is struck by a thought and pops up from the table.
The captain remains frozen.

ORLANDO

(To the audience) How odd! When I was a young man, I insisted that women be obedient, chaste and scented. Now I shall have to pay in my own person for those desires. For women are not—

CHORUS

judging by her short experience of the sex—

ORLANDO

obedient, chaste and scented by nature. They can only attain these graces by tedious discipline. There's the hairdressing . . . that alone will take at least an hour of my morning . . . there's looking in the looking-glass . . . there's being chaste year in and year out . . . Christ Jesus!

When I set foot on English soil, I shall never be able to crack a man over the head, or draw my sword and run him through the body, or lead an army . . . All I can do is to pour out tea and ask my lords how they like it.

(To the frozen captain)
D'you take sugar? D'you take cream?

CHORUS

And here she seemed to criticize both sexes
equally, as if she belonged to neither.

ORLANDO

She was a man, she was a woman—

She knew the secrets and shared the weaknesses of each.

The figure of Sasha walks past.

ORLANDO

Oh! At last I know Sasha as she really was!

CHORUS

For, though Orlando herself was a woman, it was still a woman
that she loved.

ORLANDO

And now a thousand mysteries became plain to her.

CHORUS

Her affection gained in beauty what it lost in falsity.

ORLANDO

Sasha! On legs like beech trees, grape clustered, pearl hung!
Which is the greater ecstasy? The man's or the woman's?

Sasha retreats.

ORLANDO

Don't go! I have much to tell you! And much to ask!

Sasha disappears. The captain puts his arm around Orlando.

CAPTAIN

I would like to point out to you, madam, on the horizon, gleaming
. . . the cliffs of England, madam.

ORLANDO

Christ Jesus!

CAPTAIN

The sight of her native land after so
long an absence excused her strong language.

Orlando cranes forward, looking through a telescope.

CHORUS

Ladies in flowered silk walked on footpaths.
Citizens in embroidered coats took snuff.

CAPTAIN

There you will see the Houses of Parliament—

ORLANDO

There—there had been the great carnival.

CAPTAIN

The Tower of London—

ORLANDO

There—she had first met Sasha. About here—
she had seen the frozen dolphins. All was changed.

CAPTAIN

Ah, and there, on the right, Westminster Abbey—

ORLANDO

How to tell the captain that she—

who now trembled on his arm—

had once been a duke and an ambassador . . . had hacked heads off, had lain with loose women . . .

CAPTAIN

And finally, just there, the dome of St. Paul's—

ORLANDO

Do what she would to restrain them, the tears came to Orlando's eyes, until, remembering that it is becoming in a woman to weep, she let them flow.

CAPTAIN

Dear old London. Will you need an escort, madam?

ORLANDO

No thank you, sir.

And, without anyone's assistance, she set her foot upon her native shore.

Scene 2: Orlando Returns Home.

Music from the eighteenth century.

CHORUS

It was a fine evening in December when Orlando arrived home.

Orlando alights from her carriage and sets down her luggage.

ORLANDO

Home!

The great door is flung open. A procession of servants holding torches.

MAID I *(Grimsditch)*

Milord! Milady! Milord! Milady!

ORLANDO

Orlando comforted her maid with a hearty kiss upon both cheeks.

MAID 2 *(Dupper)*

The post, my lady.

ORLANDO

Thank you.

MAID 1

If my Lord is a Lady now, I've never seen a lovelier one.

MAID 2

I've always had my suspicions.

They nod their heads mysteriously.

MAID 1

And, for my part, what with the towels needing mending, it's
high time we had a mistress.

Orlando opens a letter.

ORLANDO

No sooner had Orlando opened her mail than she discovered that
she was now victim of two major law suits:

CHORUS *(As barristers)*

1) That you are dead, and therefore cannot hold any property
whatsoever.

2) That you are a woman, which amounts to much the same thing.

ORLANDO

Christ Jesus!

Orlando sits down and reads over the letter again.
Maid 1 and Maid 2 have a conversation behind potted palms.

ORLANDO

So, while the old servants gossiped,
Orlando took a silver candle in her hand

and roamed once more through the halls,
the galleries,
the courts,
the bedrooms.
In this window seat she had written her first verses.
In that chapel, she would be buried.
She, who believed in no immortality,
could not help feeling that her soul
would come and go forever
with the reds on the panels and the greens on the sofa.
The house was no longer hers—it belonged to time now.

She sets down her candle and scrutinizes herself in the mirror.

ORLANDO

I am growing up, she thought—
I am losing some illusions, perhaps to acquire others.

She blows out her candle.

197

Scene 3: The Archduchess Harriet

Orlando writes. Her maids peer over her shoulder.

MAID 1 AND MAID 2

The next morning . . .
With fresh pen and paper,
Orlando started again upon
her *long* poem, "The Oak Tree."

ORLANDO

And then I came to a field—

A woman and her shadow pass by. Orlando looks up, startled.

CHORUS

When, suddenly, a familiar shadow . . .

ORLANDO

A grotesque shadow . . .

CHORUS

the shadow of no less than—

ARCHDUCHESS

The Archduchess Harriet Griselda of Scand-Op Boom
in Romania—

CHORUS

Appeared.

ORLANDO

(To her maids) I fled all the way to Constantinople to avoid that
fatal fowl!
A plague on women!
They never leave one a moment's peace.

Meanwhile, the Archduchess has approached and disrobes.
Underneath her fine dress she wears the clothes of a gentleman.

CHORUS

A heap of clothes lay on the ground.
In place of the Archduchess—

ARCHDUKE

(In a Romanian accent) stood a tall gentleman in black.

CHORUS

Orlando was alone with . . .

ORLANDO

A man!

Recalled thus suddenly to a consciousness of her sex, Orlando
felt seized with faintness.

La! How you frighten me!

Orlando leans back in a swoon and the Archduke catches her.

ARCHDUKE

Gentle creature, forgive me for the deceit I have practiced on you.

He kisses her hand.

ORLANDO

Indeed, it was very cruel of you to deceive me.

CHORUS

In short, they acted the parts of man and woman for ten minutes with great vigor—

Orlando swoons and the Archduke catches her.

ORLANDO

La! How you frighten me!

The Archduke chases Orlando around a table.

CHORUS

And then the two fell into natural discourse.

ARCHDUKE

Dearest lady, my story is a tragical one. (Tee-hee.) I am a man and have, indeed, always been one. (Haw-haw.) I saw a portrait of you long ago—at the time when you dressed in the stockings of a man— (Tee-hee.) —and I fell hopelessly in love with you. I knew no way of winning you but to dress as a woman. I was desolated—ruined—when you fled to Constantinople. (Haw-haw.) For to me, you were and always will be the Pink, the Pearl and the Perfection of your sex.

He kisses her hand.

ORLANDO

(To the audience) If this is love, there is something highly ridiculous about it.

The Archduke falls to his knees.

ARCHDUKE

Listen. I have more land in Romania than any nobleman in England. The shooting— (tee-hee) —is excellent. True, the pheasants have suffered from poultry disease in my absence— (haw-haw)—

ORLANDO

The peasants?

ARCHDUKE

The pheasants!—but that can be put right, my dear, and all will be well—I am certain of it—if only we lived in Romania together.

CHORUS

As he spoke,
tears ran down the sandy tracts of his cheeks.

ORLANDO

Orlando was beginning to be aware that women
should be shocked when men display
emotion in their presence, and so, shocked she was.

She slaps the Archduke.

ORLANDO

How dare you cry in my presence!

ARCHDUKE

I must apologize.
I cannot help but feel moved
to tears in the presence of your great beauty.
I must leave you now.
But I will return tomorrow for your answer to my proposition.

He kisses her hand.

CHORUS

That was a Tuesday.
He came on Wednesday.

He kisses her hand again.

CHORUS

He came on a Thursday.

He kisses her wrist.

CHORUS

And he came on a Friday . . .

He kisses her inner elbow. She slaps him.

CHORUS

Each visit began, continued, or concluded with a declaration of love:

ARCHDUKE

I love you.

ORLANDO

Thank you very much.

CHORUS

But, in between, there was much room for silence.

Orlando and the Archduke sit down next to each other.
A long silence.
The Archduke fidgets and knocks over a potted palm.
Another long silence.

ARCHDUKE

I shot an elk in Sweden.

ORLANDO

Was it a very big elk?

ARCHDUKE

Well, it was not as big as the reindeer I shot in Norway.

Silence.

ORLANDO

Have you ever shot a tiger?

ARCHDUKE

I've shot an albatross.

Orlando yawns. She looks out the window.

ORLANDO

Is an albatross as big as an elephant?

ARCHDUKE   ORLANDO
(Whispering) I adore you.   Look, it's beginning to rain.

Orlando pretends she doesn't hear and smiles brightly.
The Archduke fidgets.

ORLANDO

Will you have a cup of tea?

ARCHDUKE

Yes, please.

ORLANDO

One lump or two?

ARCHDUKE

One please . . . *(In a lower tone)* . . . my darling.

ORLANDO

Oh, I know a game! See that fly buzzing about?

ARCHDUKE

Yes.

Their eyes follow an imaginary fly circling overhead.
The chorus makes buzzing sounds.

ORLANDO

I bet you five hundred pounds that the fly will settle on *my* lump of sugar rather than on yours.

ARCHDUKE

That's a delightful game . . . my darling. I bet you five hundred pounds.

They watch the fly circle the room The fly lands on Orlando's lump of sugar.

ORLANDO

Ha ha! I've won! Five hundred pounds please!

He hands her five hundred pounds.

ORLANDO

(To the audience) What's the good of being a fine young woman in the prime of life if I have to pass all my mornings watching flies with an Archduke?

There must be some way out of this difficulty!

CHORUS

But she was still awkward in the arts of her sex, as she could no longer knock a man over the head.

ORLANDO

Orlando thought of a plan.

Oh dear, I do believe my plants are dying.

The Archduke looks at the plants.

CHORUS

While the Archduke was gazing at her plants, she gently pressed the life out of a fly.

ORLANDO

(Pressing the life out of a fly) I'm sorry little fly. There. Quite dead.

CHORUS

Her reckoning was that the Archduke
would detect the fraud, and,
as cheating is a heinous crime,
he would refuse to have anything
further to do with her.

ORLANDO

Loo! I've won again while you weren't looking! See?

ARCHDUKE

So you have, my pretty! I didn't even hear a fly buzzing about!

CHORUS

A dead fly looked to him much the same as a living one.
She played the trick twenty times and he paid
her over twenty thousand pounds.
Finally, the Archduke could be deceived
no longer.

ARCHDUKE

That fly is dead!
You killed that fly!
You pasted it onto your sugar lump!
Didn't you? Did you?

ORLANDO

Yes.

ARCHDUKE

That you won my fortune is nothing. You are welcome to it. It's only that you deceived me . . . It hurts me to think you capable of it. To love a woman who cheats at play is, I'm afraid, impossible. And yet, you are, after all, only a woman. Allowances must be made. Perhaps I can forgive you . . . out of the wildness of my passion . . .

ORLANDO

Orlando feared such a speech. And now, after concealing a toad under her blouse all morning, she dropped the toad down the shirt of the Archduke.

The Archduke howls.
Orlando laughs.

ORLANDO

She laughed.

ARCHDUKE

The Archduke blushed.

ORLANDO

She laughed!

ARCHDUKE

The Archduke cursed.

ORLANDO

She laughed.

ARCHDUKE

The Archduke slammed the door.

ORLANDO

Heaven be praised!
I am alone.

CHORUS

With the twelfth stroke of midnight,
the darkness was complete.
All was darkness
all was doubt
all was confusion.
The Eighteenth Century was over;
The Nineteenth Century had begun.

Act IV: The Nineteenth Century

Scene 1: On the Preponderance of Wedding Rings

Bells. The sound of rain.
The sound of bells gives way to the sound of many small clocks ticking.
The chorus brings baubles and trinkets on stage—doilies, curtains, a
mannequin dressed in a bustle and hat. Orlando gets dressed.

CHORUS

Rain fell frequently
but only in fitful gusts.
But what was worse—
damp now crept into every house.

Orlando enters, wearing a bustle and holding a gray umbrella. She
shakes the rain off and stands in front of the mirror.

CHORUS

And so rugs appeared;
beards were grown.
Everything was covered,

nothing was left bare.
The muffin was invented
and the crumpet.

Coffee led to a drawing room in which to drink it
and a drawing room to glass cases

and glass cases to artificial flowers
and artificial flowers to mantelpieces—

and mantelpieces to pianofortes
and (skipping a stage or two)
to innumerable little dogs, mats,
and china ornaments . . .

THE HOME was completely altered.

Orlando stands in front of the mirror, looking depressed, turning her large hat this way and that on her head.

CHORUS
Meanwhile the spirit of the age was blowing
now hot, now cold, on Orlando's cheeks.
That is, the blushes came and went with the
most exquisite degree of modesty and shame.

ORLANDO
She was becoming a little more modest of her brains
and a little more vain of her person.

CHORUS
The change of clothes had much to do with it.
Vain trifles as they seem, clothes change our view of the world and
the world's view of us. In fact, there is much to support the view
that it is the clothes that wear us and not the other way 'round.

*Orlando looks in the mirror, putting her hand to her cheeks.
The sounds of muffled chimes, wind and buzzing noises.*

ORLANDO

Orlando now became conscious
of an extraordinary tingling and vibration.
Her arms sang and twanged; her hairs seemed to erect themselves.

*Orlando begins to vibrate—first her body, then only her arms, then only
her hands, then only her left hand, then only her wedding ring finger.*

ORLANDO

All this agitation seemed at length to concentrate
in her hands, and then in one hand, and then in
one finger of that hand, and finally,
it made a ring of quivering sensibility
about the second finger of the left hand.

When Orlando raised that finger to
see what caused this agitation, she saw nothing.

CHORUS

The vibration seemed, in the oddest way, to say:
No! That is not enough.

ORLANDO

Life! A lover!

CHORUS

And the spirit of the age would always reply:
No, Orlando. Life, a husband!

ORLANDO

Until Orlando felt positively ashamed of the
second finger of her left hand without in the least
knowing why.

Orlando tries to hide her finger. Enter the maid.

ORLANDO

Let me see your hands, Grimsditch.

The maid holds out her hands—she wears a wedding ring.

ORLANDO

Let me look at your ring for a moment, Grimsditch. I'll just pull it off for a moment—

Orlando reaches for the ring. Grimsditch clutches her ring, dumbstruck.

GRIMSDITCH

No! Your Ladyship may *look* if you please, but as for taking off my wedding ring, neither the Pope nor Queen Victoria could force me to. Since my Thomas put this ring on me finger twenty-five years, six months, three weeks ago (an' that's an exact figure, Your Ladyship), I've slept in it, worked in it, washed in it, an' prayed in it. In fact, it's by the gleam on this 'ere ring that I'll be assigned my station among the angels, an' its luster would be tarnished now and forever if I let it out o' my keeping even for a wee bit.

ORLANDO

I'm sorry Grimsditch. I didn't realize. Heaven help us. What a world we live in. What a world to be sure.

Orlando takes up her umbrella and walks,
surveying the streets of London.
Wedding rings are dropped from the sky on strings.
They dangle above her.

ORLANDO

It now seemed to Orlando that the whole world was ringed in gold. She went to dinner. Wedding rings abounded.

She went to church.
Wedding rings everywhere.

Orlando could only suppose that some new discovery had been made about the race; that they were somehow stuck together, couple after couple.

Couples linked together, women leaning on men.

ORLANDO

It was strange.
Indeed—it was distasteful.

CHORUS

And yet the tingling on Orlando's left finger
persisted more violently than ever.

ORLANDO

(To her finger) Stop tingling.
I will write. I will write.

CHORUS

She picked up her manuscript—
"The Oak Tree"—

ORLANDO

She dipped her pen in ink—

CHORUS

Felt the breath of Queen Victoria on her cheek—

ORLANDO

And wrote the most insipid verse she had ever read in her life.
Oh, dear.

CHORUS

The only thing to do was to submit to
the spirit of the age
and take a husband.

ORLANDO

Whom—

CHORUS

She asked of the wild autumn winds, looking the very image of
appealing womanhood as she did so—

ORLANDO

Whom can I lean upon?

CHORUS

It was not Orlando who spoke, but the spirit of the age.

ORLANDO

I am mateless. I am alone.

CHORUS

Orlando walked over the moor, up the hill.
She picked up a feather and stuck it in her hat.
She had a wild notion of following the birds
to the rim of the world.

ORLANDO

She ran.
A strange ecstasy came over her . . .

CHORUS

And she tripped.

Orlando falls with a thud.

ORLANDO

I believe my ankle is broken.
And yet I am content.
I have found my mate.
I am nature's bride.
My hands shall wear no wedding ring.
The roots shall twine about my fingers.
I have sought happiness through many ages and not found it.
Searched for fame and missed it,
love and not known it.
I have known many men and many women,
none have I understood.
It is better that I lie in peace with thy sky above me.

She sighs. She closes her eyes.
The sound of a thumping which grows louder and more distinct until
it is the sound of a horse galloping toward her. Orlando sits upright.

ORLANDO

Orlando heard, deep within, some hammer, or was it a heart beating?

CHORUS

Tick-tock, tick-tock, so it hammered, so it beat . . .
Until it changed to the trot of horse's hoofs:
One, two three four . . .
The horse was almost upon her!

She screams.
A man comes galloping toward her, on an abstracted horse.

CHORUS

Towering against the dawn, Orlando saw a man on horseback.

MARMADUKE

Madam, you're hurt!

ORLANDO

I believe I'm dead, sir!

Marmaduke takes her in his arms. They look at each other.

ORLANDO AND MARMADUKE

A few minutes later, they became engaged.

Scene 2: The Marriage

CHORUS
The morning after, as they sat at breakfast—

ORLANDO
he told her his name.

MARMADUKE
Marmaduke Bonthrop Shelmerdine, Esquire.

ORLANDO
Marmaduke Bonthrop Shelmerdine, Esquire. I knew it!

(To the audience)
For there was something romantic and chivalrous, passionate, melancholy, yet determined about him.

(To Marmaduke)
My name is Orlando.

214

MARMADUKE

Orlando. I knew it!

For if one sees a ship in full sail proudly sweeping across the Mediterranean from the South Seas, one says at once, Orlando.

You see, though their acquaintance had been short, they had guessed, as always happens between lovers, everything of any importance about each other in two seconds at the utmost,

ORLANDO

and it now remained only to fill in such unimportant details as what they were called,

MARMADUKE

where they lived,

ORLANDO

and whether or not they were beggars.
You're not a beggar, are you Shel?

MARMADUKE

I once had a castle, but it was ruined. So I became a—

ORLANDO	MARMADUKE
Sailor!	Sailor.

MARMADUKE

How did you know?

ORLANDO

I guessed it. And the winds—they went the wrong way suddenly?

MARMADUKE

Yes-yes—the wind went violently the wrong way, so I . . .

MARMADUKE	ORLANDO
stopped for the night.	stopped for the night.

MARMADUKE

Yes! And, I'm due to leave for the South Seas tomorrow.

Pause.

ORLANDO

Tomorrow! Oh, Shel, don't leave me! I'm in love with you!

MARMADUKE

No sooner had the words left her mouth than an awful suspicion rushed into both their minds at once.

MARMADUKE	ORLANDO
You're a man, Orlando!	You're a woman, Shel!

ORLANDO

You think . . . you think I'm a man? Oh, no, I'm very much a woman.

MARMADUKE

And you, for a moment, thought I was a woman? How ridiculous.

But you're so entirely *sympathetic*—and you never take more than ten minutes to dress—how can it be—

ORLANDO

And you have a passion for—peppermints, and you blush so easily. How can it be—

And they talked two hours or more, perhaps about the sea or perhaps *not* about the sea, and really it would profit little to record what they said, for they knew each other so well that they could say anything, which is tantamount to saying nothing.

MARMADUKE

Once I was sailing the South Seas and was caught in a *terrific* gale. Masts were snapped off, sails were torn to ribbons . . .

ORLANDO

Christ Jesus! How exciting! Then what?

MARMADUKE

The ship sank, and I was left, the only survivor, on a raft holding
a biscuit.

ORLANDO

And?

MARMADUKE

I ate the biscuit. It's about all a fellow can do nowadays . . .

Orlando laughs.

MARMADUKE

Are you positive you aren't a man?

ORLANDO

Can it be possible you're not a woman?

MARMADUKE AND ORLANDO

And then they must put it to the proof without more ado.

They kiss passionately.

MARMADUKE

When it was over, Orlando had tears in her eyes—

ORLANDO

Tears of a finer flavor than any she had cried before.
I am a woman.
A real woman at last.

Thank you, Shel, for this rare and unexpected delight.

MARMADUKE

You're welcome, Orlando.

ORLANDO

For each was so surprised at the quickness of the other's sympathy,

and it was to each such a revelation that

MARMADUKE

a woman could be as
tolerant and free-spoken as a man,

ORLANDO

and a man as strange and subtle as a woman.

MARMADUKE

So they would talk.

ORLANDO

And talk.

MARMADUKE

How to cook an omelette—

ORLANDO

Where to buy the best boots in London—

MARMADUKE

Yes—

ORLANDO

Yes.

MARMADUKE

And when Orlando's feet were covered with spotted autumn leaves . . .

ORLANDO

Bonthrop . . .

MARMADUKE

she would say . . .

ORLANDO

I'm off.

MARMADUKE

When she called him his second name—

ORLANDO

Bonthrop—

MARMADUKE

it should signify that she was in a solitary mood, felt them both as specks on a desert—

ORLANDO

for people die daily, die at dinner tables or out of doors in the autumn leaves, and so saying:
Bonthrop . . .

MARMADUKE

she said in effect,

ORLANDO

"I'm dead."

The sound of the sea.
A terrible stillness.

MARMADUKE

After some hours of death
usually a bird would shriek:

CHORUS

Shelmerdine!

MARMADUKE

and she would come to life again . . .

ORLANDO

as though returning from a voyage
on a ship which had heaved and tossed
and finally rides over the crest of a wave . . .

Shelmerdine!

MARMADUKE

What is it, Orlando?

ORLANDO

It's passed now. I'm alive, darling Shel.

ORLANDO AND MARMADUKE

Until one day,
They got married.

The sound of bells.

CHORUS

Bells were rung!
People were summoned!

ORLANDO AND MARMADUKE

The rain poured down on them!

CHORUS

They reached the chapel,
light flew through the painted windows . . .

A PRIEST

Marmaduke Bonthrop Shelmerdine and Lady Orlando, kneel down.

They kneel.
The lights go on and off.
The sound of doors banging,
brass pots beating, and an organ sounding.

CHORUS

All was confusion!
Now a bird was dashed against a pane,
now there was a clap of thunder!

A clap of thunder.

ORLANDO

(Shouting over the noise) So that no one heard the word Obey—

MARMADUKE

or saw a ring pass from hand to hand.

ORLANDO

(Shouting over the noise) Marmaduke Bonthrop Shelmerdine, Esquire!

MARMADUKE

Orlando!

CHORUS

And the words went dashing and circling
like wild hawks among the towers,
faster and faster they circled,
until they crashed and
fell in a shower of fragments to the ground.

The Twentieth Century had arrived.

The sound of tinkling glass.

Act V: The Twentieth Century

Scene 1

The sound of a clock ticking louder and louder.
The chorus hops into an imaginary car.
Orlando changes into a costume with twentieth century proportions.

ORLANDO

Look at that!
A carriage without any horses, indeed!
It's an odd sort of weather nowadays.

CHORUS

The sky itself had changed.
The sky seemed made of metal.
The clouds had shrunk to a thin gauze.
It was harder to cry now.
Vegetables were less fertile;
Families much smaller.

ORLANDO

Everything, in fact, seemed to have shrunk.
It was more than a little alarming.

The stage brightens.

ORLANDO

And look! The lights in the houses! Hundreds of little rooms are
lit, one precisely the same as the other. One can see everything
in the little square-shaped boxes; there seems to be no privacy—
none of those lingering shadows that there used to be, none of
those women in aprons carrying wobbly lamps.

At a touch, the whole room is bright!

Orlando experiments with a light switch. She turns the light off and on.

ORLANDO

And the sky is bright all night long!

CHORUS

The clock ticked louder and louder until there was a terrific
explosion in Orlando's ear.

The lights go completely bright—to morning brightness.

ORLANDO

Orlando leapt as if she had been violently struck on the head. Ten
times she was struck. In fact, it was ten o'clock in the morning.
It was:

EVERYONE

the present moment.

CHORUS

No one need wonder that Orlando pressed her hand to her heart
and turned pale.

For what more terrifying revelation can there be than that it is the present moment?
That we survive the shock at all is only possible because the past shelters us on one side and the future on the other—

ORLANDO

But we have no time now for such reflections.

CHORUS

Orlando was terribly late.

ORLANDO

She jumped into her motor-car.

Orlando jumps into an imaginary motor-car.

CHORUS

Vast blue blocks of buildings rose into the air.
She noticed sponges,
bird cages,
boxes of green American cloth.
Here was a market,
here was a funeral.
Meat was very red.

ORLANDO

But Orlando did not allow these sights to sink
into her mind even the fraction of an inch—

Orlando honks her horn.

ORLANDO

Why don't you look where you're going!

CHORUS

For the streets were immensely crowded.
People buzzed and hummed everywhere,
as if they were bees.

225

Orlando honks her horn again.

ORLANDO
Why don't you look where you're going!

CHORUS
Orlando jumped out of her car,
rushed into a large department store,
and got into the lift.

Everyone crowds into the lift. The sound of an elevator ding.

ORLANDO
This must be middle-age.

ELEVATOR MAN
Four . . .

ORLANDO
Time has passed over me.

ELEVATOR MAN
Six—

ORLANDO
How strange it is! Nothing is any longer one thing. I take up a
handbag and think of a porpoise frozen beneath the sea. Someone
lights a pink candle and I see a girl in Russian trousers.

ELEVATOR MAN
Seven—

ORLANDO
I hear goat bells. I see mountains. But where? Turkey? India?
Persia? I can't think . . .

ELEVATOR MAN
Linens . . .

The elevator door opens. Everyone rushes out.
Orlando finds a salesperson.

ORLANDO

I need sheets for a double bed.

SALESPERSON

Yes, ma'am.

The salesperson looks through sheets. Orlando spots herself in a mirror.

ORLANDO

I scarcely look a day older! I look just as rosy as I did that day on the ice, when the Thames was frozen and we had gone skating . . .

Sasha appears.

SASHA

You are like a million-candled Christmas tree such as we have in Russia—

ORLANDO

Sasha!

SASHA

enough to light a whole street by.

ORLANDO

Is it you, Sasha?

SASHA

And the figure walked through swinging doors, a whiff of scent as though from pink candles following her figure—

ORLANDO

Was it a boy's figure or was it a girl's?

SASHA

Young, slender, seductive . . .

227

ORLANDO

A girl, by God! Furred, pearled, in Russian trousers, but faithless!
Faithless! Oh, Sasha, why?

SALESPERSON

The best Irish linen, ma'am.

Sasha disappears into the crowd.

SALESPERSON

Any napkins, towels, or dusters today, ma'am?

ORLANDO

There's only one thing in the world I want today, and that is bath
salts.

SALESPERSON

You'll want to take the lift to the first floor, ma'am.

ORLANDO

Thank you very much.

Orlando leaves.

SALESPERSON

Your bedsheets, ma'am!

Orlando enters the elevator—the sound of an elevator ding.

CHORUS

And can we blame her for forgetting her bedsheets, when she was
actually hundreds of years old?
For the true length of a person's life is always a matter of dispute.
Of some we can justly say that they live precisely the sixty-eight
years allotted them on the tombstone. Others are hundreds of
years old though we call them thirty-six.
It is a difficult business, this time-keeping, and nothing more
quickly disorders time than contact with any of the arts . . .

The elevator dings and the doors sweep open.

ORLANDO

Confound it all! I've forgotten the bedsheets! No matter. I want,
more than anything, to go home.

CHORUS

Without her bedsheets
or her bath salts,
Orlando hopped into her motor-car.

ORLANDO

Nothing could be seen whole or read from start
to finish. She saw signs—

Cadbu . . . Cadburg—Cadbury . . . Choc . . . Choc-ates
Ra—Rall against unemp . . . ent
Applejohn Under—tkr . . .

CHORUS

And it flashed by, unread.

ORLANDO

What one saw beginning—

CHORUS

like two friends starting to meet each other
across the street—

ORLANDO

was never seen ended.

CHORUS

After ten minutes the body and mind
were like scraps of torn paper
tumbling from a sack.

She motored out of London
so entirely disassembled

that it is an open question as to whether
she existed at all.

Orlando screeches into her own driveway.

ORLANDO

Orlando walked into her house
and called, Orlando!
Orlando! Come here! I'm sick to death of
this particular self. I want another. Orlando?

CHORUS

For she had a great variety of selves to call upon:
the boy who sat under the oak tree,
the young man who fell in love with Sasha,
the boy who handed the Queen a bowl of rose water,
the poet, the fine lady,
the woman who called Mar
or Shelmerdine
or Bonthrop—

ORLANDO

Orlando! Haunted, haunted, ever since I was a child. Flinging
a net of words after the wild goose of meaning and everything
shrivels . . . Orlando?

CHORUS

Still, the Orlando that she wanted did not come.

ORLANDO

All right then.

The chorus disappears.

ORLANDO

(To the audience)
Who then am I?

Thirty-six, owns a motor-car, a woman. Yes—but a million other things as well. Am I a snob? Proud of my ancestors?

Don't give a damn if I am. Truthful? I think so. Generous? Oh, but that doesn't count. Spoilt? Perhaps. Clumsy? Absolutely.

I love trees. And barns. And the night. But people. People? I don't know. Chattering, spiteful, always telling lies.

And, yet . . . love—what of it? Flies on the ceiling? Sasha? Marmaduke?

CHORUS
The great wings of silence beat up and down the empty house. All was lit as if for the coming of a dead queen.

Enter Queen Elizabeth.
Orlando kneels at her feet and kisses her hands.

ORLANDO
The house is at your service, Mum. Nothing has been changed.

THE QUEEN
What's wrong, Orlando?

ORLANDO
Wrong?

THE QUEEN
You don't seem like yourself.

ORLANDO
I'm not sure that there is such a thing, Your Highness.

THE QUEEN
Don't be silly, Orlando. You are many things, to many people. To me, you are a boy with delightful legs in silk stockings—apparently you have changed. But no matter. The dead have wonderful memories.

ORLANDO

I would like, Your Highness, at the present moment, to feel as though I am only one thing.

THE QUEEN

Poppycock! Don't be a bore, Orlando. You were never a bore in silk stockings.

ORLANDO

What is death like, Your Highness?

THE QUEEN

Oh, that. Nothing really, just a prick in the sides. My sinuses are *unbelievably* clear. All is air.

ORLANDO

I long for death at moments . . .

THE QUEEN

You've always been morbid. And yet, when I knew you, Orlando, you were filled with life—exquisitely—you were bursting with it.

ORLANDO

I remember.

THE QUEEN

Perhaps it's the spirit of the age.

ORLANDO

Perhaps. We don't know why we go upstairs or why we come down again—our most daily movements are like the passage of a ship on an unknown sea.

THE QUEEN

(Pointing) Look, Orlando, there is the wild goose—in the garden.

ORLANDO

Where?

THE QUEEN

Just there—

ORLANDO

The wild goose—and the secret of life is . . . ?

THE QUEEN

(Turning to go) A small kiss, for old time's sake?

Orlando kisses the Queen. The Queen exits.

ORLANDO

Orlando banished these thoughts. She remembered with a start that she was married. Shelmerdine?

CHORUS

She was married, true, but if one's husband was always sailing around the world, was that marriage?

ORLANDO

And if one liked him, was it marriage? If one liked other people, was it marriage?

CHORUS

And finally . . . most importantly . . .

ORLANDO

If one still wished, more than anything in the whole world, to write poetry, was it marriage?

CHORUS

She had her doubts.

ORLANDO

But she would put it to the test.

CHORUS

She flung herself under the old oak tree.
She took up her poem.

ORLANDO

Seastained, bloodstained, travelstained—

CHORUS

She had been working on it for close on five hundred years now.

ORLANDO

She looked at the ring.
She looked at the inkpot—

CHORUS

Did she dare?

ORLANDO

Hang it all! Here goes!

CHORUS

And she plunged her pen neck deep in ink. To her enormous surprise, she wrote. The words were a little long in coming, but come they did.

She writes.

CHORUS

And all the time she was writing, the world continued . . .
through wars
and other calamities . . .

ORLANDO

She listened for the sound of gunfire at sea—

CHORUS

No, only the wind blew.

ORLANDO

There is no war today.

CHORUS

And so—she wrote.

She looks up.

ORLANDO

What's life?
she asked a bird.

CHORUS

Life, life, life, cried the bird!

Orlando keeps writing. The chorus looks on.

CHORUS

Finally, Orlando dropped her pen and stretched her arms.

ORLANDO

Done! Done! It's done!

CHORUS

And the poem wanted to be read.
Human beings had become necessary.

ORLANDO

Yes—

CHORUS

The first stroke of midnight sounded.
The cold breeze of the present brushed her face
with its little breath of fear.

ORLANDO

Shelmerdine! Here, Shel, here I am!

She waves to Shel who appears at a distance. He moves toward her.
The clock continues to chime twelve times.

ORLANDO

He came, as he always did, in moments of dead calm—

CHORUS

When the wave rippled, the spotted leaves fell slowly—
and nothing moved between sky and sea.

ORLANDO

Then he came.

MARMADUKE

Orlando!

ORLANDO

Shelmerdine!

CHORUS

And the twelfth stroke of midnight sounded—
it was, in fact,
the present moment.
Orlando's mind began to toss like the sea.

The faint sounds of the modern world—a muffled airplane, a war, a computer, a telephone.

ORLANDO

I can begin to live again.
The little boat is climbing through the white arch
of a thousand deaths.

I am about to understand . . .

Lights fade out.
The end.

Acknowledgments

MANY PEOPLE ASSISTED ME in translating *Three Sisters* (especially given my very great handicap of not knowing Russian). The greatest among these were Elise Thoron and Natasha Paramonova, my sister-in-law. I am grateful to the visionary John Doyle for giving the translation its first life, to that indelible cast, and to Ed Stern for commissioning the piece. I am also incredibly grateful to my long-time collaborators Les Waters and Joyce Piven for mounting the translation again so beautifully, and to Berkeley Repertory Theatre, Yale Repertory Theatre and the Piven Theatre Workshop for housing those productions. Thank you to Keith Reddin for living with Kulygin so long. Thanks also to New Dramatists, which hosted the very first hearing of the translation, and also hosted a workshop of *Orlando*.

As for *Orlando*: thank you to Joyce Piven for commissioning the adaptation and for trusting me so early in life with such a task. Thanks also for her beautiful productions in Chicago and in L.A., and to Polly Noonan for creating Orlando so memorably. Thank you to Rebecca Taichman and Jessica Thebus for reimagining the play, and to those glorious ensembles. (David Greenspan—your Queen Elizabeth attire is forever in my living room.)

SARAH RUHL's plays include *In the Next Room or the vibrator play* (Pulitzer Prize finalist, Tony Award nominee, Best Play); *The Clean House* (Pulitzer Prize finalist, Susan Smith Blackburn Prize); *Passion Play, a cycle* (Pen American Award, The Fourth Freedom Forum Playwriting Award from The Kennedy Center); *Dead Man's Cell Phone* (Helen Hayes Award); *Melancholy Play*; *Eurydice*; *Orlando*; *Demeter in the City* (NAACP nomination); *Late: a cowboy song* and, most recently, *Dear Elizabeth* and *Stage Kiss*. Her plays have been produced on Broadway at the Lyceum Theatre by Lincoln Center Theater; Off-Broadway at Playwrights Horizons, Second Stage and Lincoln Center's Mitzi Newhouse Theater. They have also been produced across the country, often premiering at Yale Repertory Theatre, Berkeley Repertory Theatre and the Goodman. Originally from Chicago, Ms. Ruhl received her MFA from Brown University where she studied with Paula Vogel. In 2003, she was the recipient of the Helen Merrill Emerging Playwrights Award and the Whiting Writers' Award. She was a member of 13P and of New Dramatists and won the MacArthur Fellowship in 2006. You can read more about her work on www.SarahRuhlplaywright.com. She teaches playwriting at the Yale School of Drama, and she lives in Brooklyn with her family.